P9-DIE-281

THE COLOR MASTER

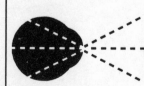

This Large Print Book carries the
Seal of Approval of N.A.V.H.

THE COLOR MASTER

STORIES

AIMEE BENDER

THORNDIKE PRESS
A part of Gale, Cengage Learning

GALE
CENGAGE Learning®

Detroit • New York • San Francisco • New Haven, Conn • Waterville, Maine • London

GALE
CENGAGE Learning®

LIBRARY OF CONGRESS CATALOGING-IN-PUBLICATION DATA

Bender, Aimee.
  [Short stories. Selections]
  The color master : stories / by Aimee Bender. — Large print edition.
    pages ; cm. — (Thorndike Press large print basic)
  ISBN-13: 978-1-4104-6511-5 (hardcover)
  ISBN-10: 1-4104-6511-X (hardcover)
  1. Large type books. I. Title.
  PS3552.E538447A6 2013
  813'.54—dc23   2013035077

Published in 2014 by arrangement with Doubleday, an imprint of Knopf Doubleday Publishing Group, a division of Random House, Inc.

for Mark

CONTENTS

■ ■ ■ ■

PART ONE

■ ■ ■ ■

APPLELESS

I once knew a girl who wouldn't eat apples. She wove her walking around groves and orchards. She didn't even like to look at them. They're all mealy, she said. Or else too cheeky, too bloomed. *No,* she stated again, in case we had not heard her, our laps brimming with Granny Smiths and Red Deliciouses. With Galas and Spartans and yellow Golden Globes. But we had heard her, from the very first; we just couldn't help offering again. Please, we pleaded, eat. Cracking our bites loudly, exposing the dripping wet white inside.

It's unsettling to meet people who don't eat apples.

The rest of us now eat only apples, to compensate. She has declared herself so apple-less, we feel we have no other choice. We sit in the orchard together, cross-legged, and when they fall off the trees into our outstretched hands, we bite right in. They are pale green, striped red-on-red, or a yellow-and-orange sunset. They are the threaded Fujis, with streaks of woven jade and beige, or the dark and rosy Rome Beauties. Pippins, Pink Ladies, Braeburns, McIntosh. The orchard grows them all.

We suck water off the meat. Drink them dry. We pick apple skin out from the spaces between our teeth. We eat the stem and the seeds. For the moment, there are enough beauties bending the branches for all of us to stay fed. We circle around the core, teeth busy, and while we chew, we watch the girl circle our orchard, in her long swishing skirts, eyes averted.

One day we see her, and it's too much. She is so beautiful on this day, her skin as wide and open as a river. We could swim right down her. It's unbearable just to let her walk off, and all at once, we abandon our laps of apples and run over. Her hair is so long and wheatlike you could bake it into bread. For a second our hearts pang, for bread. Bread! We've been eating only apples now for weeks.

We close in; we ring her. Her lips fold into each other; our lips skate all over her throat, her bare wrists, her empty palms. We kiss her like we've been starving, and she tilts her head down so she doesn't have to look

12

at us. We knead her hair and kiss down the long line of her leg beneath the shift of her skirt. We pray to her, and our breath is ripe with apple juice. You can see the tears start races down her face while our hands move in to touch the curve of her breasts and the scoop of her neckline. She is so new. There are pulleys in her skin. Our fingers, all together, work their way to her bare body, past the voluminous yards of cloth. Past those loaves of hair. We find her in there, and she is so warm and so alive and we see the tears, but stop? Impossible. We breathe in, closer. Her eyelashes brighten with water. Her shoulders tremble like doves. She is weeping into our arms, she is crumpling down, and we are inside her clothes now, and our hands and mouths are everywhere. There's no sound at all but the slip of skin and her crying and the apples in the orchard thumping, uncaught: our lunches and dinners and breakfasts. It's an unfamiliar sound, because for weeks now, we have not let even one single fruit hit dirt.

She cries through it all, and when we're done and piled around her, suddenly timid and spent, suddenly withered nothings, she is the first to stand. She gathers her skirts around herself, and smooths back down her hair. She wipes her eyes clear and folds her hands around her waist. She is away from the orchard before we can stand properly and beg her to stay. Before we can grovel and claw at her small perfect feet. We watch her walk, and she's slow and proud, but none of us can possibly catch her. We splay on the ground in heaps instead as she gets smaller and smaller on the horizon.

She never comes by the orchard again, and in a week, all the apples are gone. They fall off the trees, and the trees make no new ones. The air smells like snow on the approach. No one dares to mention her, but every morning, all of our eyes are fixed on the road, waiting, hoping, staring through the bare brambles of an empty orchard. Our stomachs rumble, hungry. The sky is always this same sort of blue. It is so beautiful here.

THE RED RIBBON

It began with his fantasy, told to her one night over dinner and wine at L'Oiseau d'Or, a French restaurant with tiny gold birds etched into every plate and bowl.

"My college roommates," he said, during the entrée. "Once brought home."

"Drugs?"

"Women," said Daniel softly, "that they paid for." Even in candlelight, she could track the rise of his blush.

"Prostitutes?" Janet said. "Is that what you mean? They did?"

The kitchen doors swung open as the waiter brought a feathery dessert to the table next to theirs.

"I did not join in, Janet," Daniel said, reaching over to clasp her hand tightly. "Never. Not once. But I sometimes think about the idea of it. Not really it, itself —"

"The idea of it."

"I never once joined in," Daniel repeated.

"I believe you," said Janet, crossing her legs. She wondered what the handsome couple sharing the chocolate mousse would make of this conversation, even though they were laughing closely with each other and seemed to have no need for anyone else in the restaurant. She herself had noticed everyone else in the restaurant while waiting for the pâté to arrive, dressed in its sprig of parsley: the older couple, the lanky waiter, the women wrapped in patterned scarves. Now she felt like propelling herself into one of their conversations.

"I'm upsetting you," he said, swirling fork lines into his white sauce.

"Not so much," she said.

"Never mind," he said. "Really. You look so beautiful tonight, Janet."

On the drive home, she sat in the back-seat, as she did on occasion. He said it was to protect her from more dangerous car accidents; she liked thinking for a moment that he was her chauffeur, that she had reached a state of adult richness where you did nothing for yourself anymore and returned to infancy. She imagined she had a cook, a hairdresser, a bath-filler. A woman who came over to fluff her pillow and tuck her in. Daniel turned on the classical music station and a cello concerto spilled out from

16

the speakers in the back, and from the angle of her seat, Janet could just catch a glimpse of the bottom of her nose and top of her lips in the rearview mirror. She stared at them for the entire ride home. Her nose had fine small bones at the tip, and her lipstick, even after dinner, was unsmudged. There was something deeply soothing to her in this image, in the simplicity of her vanity. She liked how her upper lip fit inside her lower lip, and she liked the distance between the bottom of her nose and the top of her mouth. She liked the curve of her ear. And in those likings and their basic balance, she felt herself take shape as Daniel drove.

Back at home, she spent longer than usual in the bathroom, suddenly rediscovering all the lotion bottles in the cabinet that were custom-made for different parts of the body. For feet, for elbows, for eyes, for the throat. Like different kinds of soil that need to be tilled with different tools. When she entered the bedroom, fully cultivated, skin stenciled by a lace nightgown, the lights were off. Only the moon through the window revealed the tiny triangles of skin beneath the needlework.

"Time for bed, honey," she said cheerily, which was code for *Don't touch me.* But there was no real need; his back already radiated the grainy warmth of sleeping skin. She slid herself between the sheets and called up another picture, this one of Daniel, a green bill wrapped around his erection like a condom. The itch of the corners of the bill as they pricked inside her. His stuff all over the faces of presidents. Stop it now, Janet, she thought to herself, but she finally had to take a pill to get the image out of her head; it made her too jittery to sleep.

Daniel went to work at the shoe company in the morning, suit plus vest, and Janet slept in, as usual. Her afternoons were wide open. Today, after she had wrested all the hot water out of the shower, she went straight to a lingerie shop to buy a black bustier. She remained in the dressing room for over twenty minutes, staring at her torso shoveled into the satin.

"So, Janet," called the saleslady, Tina, younger and suppler, "is it lovely? Does it fit?"

Janet pulled her sweater on and went up to the counter.

"It fit," she said, "and I'm wearing it home. How much?"

Tina, now at the cash register, snapped a garter belt between her fingers. "I need the little tag," she said. "This isn't like a shoe store."

Janet inhaled to full height, had some trouble breathing out because her ribs were smashed together, and said, sharply: "Give me the price, Tina. I will not remove this piece of clothing now that it's on, so I either pay for it this way or walk out the door with it on for free."

When she left the store, emboldened, receipt tucked into her purse, folded twice, Janet thought of all the chicken dishes she had not sent back even though they were either half-raw or not what she had ordered. Chicken Kiev instead of chicken Marsala, chicken with mushrooms instead of chicken à la king: her body was made up of the wrong chickens. She remembered Daniel's first insistent kiss, by the bridge near the Greek café on that Saturday afternoon, and she hadn't thought of it in years and she could almost smell the shawarma rotating on its pole outside. He had asked her out again, and again, and told her he loved her on the fourth date, and bought her fancy cards inside of which he wrote long messages about her smile.

By seven o'clock that night, all the shoes in Daniel's shoe store were either sold or back in boxes, and clip-clop-clip came his own up the walkway. The sky was dimming from dark blue into black, and Janet sat in the warmly lit hallway, legs crossed, bustier pressing her breasts out like beach balls, the little hooks fastened one notch off in the back so that she seemed a bit crooked.

Daniel paused in the doorway with his briefcase. "Oh my," he said, "what's this?"

She felt her upper lip twitching. "Hello, Daniel," she said. "Welcome home."

She stood awkwardly and approached him. She tried to remember: Be slow. Don't rush. When she had removed his coat and vest and laid them evenly on the floor, she reached into the back of his pants and pulled out his walnut-colored wallet. He watched, eyes huge, as she sifted through the bills until she found what she wanted. That smart Mr. Franklin.

He usually used the hundred-dollar bill to buy his best friend, Edward from business school, a lunch with fine wine on their sports day.

She waved it in his face.

"Okay?" she said.

He grabbed her waist as she tucked the bill inside the satin between her breasts.

"Janet?" he said.

She pushed him onto the carpet and began to take off the rest of his clothes.

Halfway through the buttons on his shirt, right at his ribs, she was filled with an enormous terror and had to stop to catch her breath.

"For a week, Daniel," she whispered, trembling. "Each time. Okay? Promise?"

His breathing was sharp and tight. "A week," he said, adding figures fast in his head. "Of course, I would love a week, a week," and his words floated into murmur as she drove her body into his.

They forgot about dinner. They stayed at that spot on the carpet for hours and then tumbled off to the bedroom, his coat and vest resting flat on the carpet. He stroked the curve of her neck with the light-brown mole. She fell asleep first.

On Wednesday, Janet heard Daniel call Edward and cancel their lunch date. "I'm just too busy this week," he said. Janet smiled to herself in the bathtub. He brought her handfuls of daffodils. "My wife doesn't love me," he told her in bed, which made her laugh from the deep bottom of her throat. She put a flower between her teeth and danced for him, naked, singing too loud. He grabbed her and pushed her into chairs and she kept singing, as loud as she possibly could, straddling him, wiggling, until finally he clamped a hand over her mouth and she bit his palm and slapped his thighs until they flushed pink. When it was over she felt she'd shared something fearfully intimate with him and could barely look him in the eye, but he just handed her the hundred and went into the bathroom.

On their wedding day, Daniel had given her a card with a photograph of a beach on it. "You are my fantasy woman," he'd written inside. "You come to me from my dreams." It had annoyed her then, like a bug on her arm. I come to you from Michigan, she had told him. From 928 Washington Street. He'd laughed. "That's what I love so much about you, Janet," he'd said, whirling her onto the dance floor. "You're no-nonsense," he'd said. She'd spent the song trying furtively to imitate Edward's wife, who danced like she had the instruments buzzing inside her hips.

By the end of the week, nine hundred dollars nestled in her underwear drawer. She put the bills on the ironing board and flattened them out, faces up, until they were so crisp they could be in a salad.

She'd thought about buying a dress. My whore dress! she'd thought. She considered sixty lipsticks. My hooker lips! she thought.

22

Finally she just tucked the cash into her purse and took herself to lunch. Thirty dollars brought her to the best bistro in the area, where she had a hamburger and a glass of wine. The juice dripped down, red-brown, and left a stain on her wrist.

"Ah, fuck you," she said to the homeless man on the street who asked for change. "You really think I can spare any of my NINE HUNDRED DOLLARS that I made by SELLING MY BODY?"

The man shook his head to the ground. "Sorry, ma'am," he said. "I never would have guessed."

"And don't you God-bless me!" she yelled at the man from down the block.

"I will not," he called back. "I have no interest in blessing you at all."

Once she was home she couldn't bear to sit down. She couldn't move or answer the phone. Breathing felt like an enormous burden.

She took an hour getting dressed in a pressed slate-gray suit she'd never worn before but had bought because it was on sale and elegantly cut. The jacket had this slight flare. She swept her hair into a bun and clasped a pearl necklace from their fifth wedding anniversary around her throat. Daniel came home, and she served him rosemary lamb and chocolate-nut truffles, all bought at the gourmet food store with one hundred dollars of her money. Reinvest for greater profit later. She did not eat, but massaged his shoulders, and brought him coffee, and when he seemed calm and satisfied, she sat down with him at the table.

"You're being so loving," he said. "What a week we had, didn't we?" He warmed his palms against the mug. "And you look great in that suit, Janet. Like one hot businesswoman."

She set a piece of paper on the table. And then nodded, as if to signal herself to begin.

"I know it's odd," she said, with no introduction, "but for whatever reason, I can't seem to summon up any desire right now to do it without payment." Her voice was the same one from the lingerie store when she'd walked out with the bustier on. "I need a specific amount, each time," she said, "or," clearing her throat, "I feel I will melt into nothingness." She adjusted the cuffs of her suit jacket so that the buttons lined up right with the gateway into her hand.

"What's that paper?"

"Just for notes."

"Are you going somewhere later?" he asked, sipping his coffee.

"Did you hear what I said?"

"I'm getting to that," he said. "You're just all dressed up, I was trying now to figure out why."

"I'm not going anywhere," she said coldly. "I dressed up for you."

He replaced his coffee in the center of the small white napkin. "Well, you look very nice," he said. "As usual. But, Janet," he said, "please, will you tell me why more money, why? If it's to please me, I am so pleased. You and I had a wonderful time this week, and I will remember it forever."

"Me too," she said, nodding. "Forever."

"But, then, why more money?" he asked, moving his chair closer to her. "Wasn't it just a game? Don't you like our sex? Isn't sex its own reward? What can we do differently?"

He reached out his hand, warm from cupping the mug, and placed it on her collarbone, tracing the line with his finger.

"It's good," Janet said briskly, "I like it, I like how you touch me on my back, I like the pace and the kissing, and I like it." Daniel moved his finger to the dip at the hollow of her throat, but her voice did not shift or relax. "But Daniel," she continued, "let me make something clear. Maybe you did not know this, but nothing is its own reward for me." She stared at his face as directly as she

25

could. The words felt like fireballs in her mouth. "I want you to understand that. You don't have to understand why, just that it's true."

"That nothing is its own reward? Really?"

She sat up straighter. "Now, we can of course reduce the fee to make it more financially feasible. Fifty?"

He took his hand off her body and placed it back on the table. "I mean, Janet," he said, "do you have any idea how hard I am working my ass off to make —"

"Twenty?" she said. "I know you're working so hard, honey, I know. But it would mean so much to me." As soon as her voice softened, it began to break apart. "I can hardly explain how much it means to me."

"Twenty?" he said. "Twenty?" He stuck out his lower lip, thinking. "Twenty? Jesus. I suppose I could do twenty for another week, but I don't like it. I don't want to. And is nothing its own reward, Janet? Really? Isn't love its own reward?"

"Or thirty?" she asked, sorry now that she'd gone so low.

"Twenty, Janet," said Daniel. "And then come on, now. How much money can you really make in a week off twenty dollars? Do you have something you need to buy and don't want to tell me about? Do you think you should reconsider going back to work?"

"Twenty-five?" she murmured, tears in her eyes.

He sipped the last of his coffee very slowly, and when her eyes spilled he leaned in to kiss her forehead. "Twenty-five," he said. "Fine. Until November 1, though, and then we're back to regular. Okay?"

"November 8?" she asked, brushing dry her cheeks.

"Janet!"

She moved closer and pressed him desperately to her. "Our love is wonderful," she said. "I know that. I know it's true."

His nose pushed into the smoothness of her hair. "We're each other's reward," he offered, but she just dug her head deeper into his shoulder and whispered into the caves of his neck.

"November 8, then," he said. "And that's it-it-it."

"Thank you, Daniel," she breathed. "You have no idea."

After they hugged, he went to watch TV. She wrote it all down carefully on the paper: *November 8. 25 dollars. 770 currently.* As if she would forget.

Starting the next morning, she initiated sex

every day. If the week before had been largely his fantasy enacted, now it was all hers. In the shower, in the darkness under all the covers of the bed, at his warehouse among the shoeboxes in his work boots. It felt slightly pathetic to her that she had to do four now to each one before to make the same amount of cash, but she was ravenously hungry for contact all day long, and Daniel, who had grown accustomed — before the previous week — to a steady but slightly lackluster sex life, let her enthusiasm spark his own. He took a lunch with Edward as a break, and only begged fatigue a few times when Janet's demand was kind of overwhelming, he said, since he'd just gotten home and just this morning in the shower and he needed some food and couldn't they watch TV tonight?

She laughed with big red smudge-free lips and fed him and let him watch four sitcoms in a row, but before he fell asleep she was on him again and said he didn't have to do anything at all but just be still and sleepy and she would complete all the movement.

At the end of the week, on Sunday afternoon, she presented him with a tidy bill, typewritten, accounting for each time, and labeling where/when it had happened, with a dotted line and a *$25* at the end. The total for that first week was $250. A small amount compared with the easy near-thousand of the previous week, but a clear exchange nonetheless. Daniel paid it into her palm, in cash, counting backwards.

"Sunday's my day off," he said when she started to undo her bra. "Go do something else, honey, please." He plopped in front of the TV with a bowl of rice cereal to watch some football, and Janet gathered herself into the pale-blue bathtub and attended to her body quietly in there, moaning softly under the whir of the bathroom fan; afterward, she paid herself fifty dollars by transferring funds from her savings to her checking account. That made three hundred dollars for the week.

November 8 shot around the corner in a blink; it was probably the quickest two weeks of her life. And it was not enough. That much was clear instantly. She had started, by now, to see the entire world in terms of currencies. She considered charging her few friends for their lunches based on who demanded more time and attention during the lunch itself, charging strangers a quarter in the supermarket aisle when they did not move their cart in time. Charging for each meal she cooked, including tip. One afternoon, when her father sailed off into one of his long monologues on the phone, she actually tape-recorded their conversation and then took four hours and typed it out as a script, with his endless speech on the right side of the page and her responses on the left: yes, uh-huh, of course. It was amazing, to see the contrast. How long were those pageful reports. How little she spoke. How wealthy she would be if she just charged him a dollar a word.

I am twenty-four-hour resentment, said Janet, in her bustier, to the glinting mirror. I am every-cell resentment. I am one hell of a big resentment, she said. The mirror and wall did not answer. They knew very well what she was like by now. But when had it shifted? In high school, she'd walked tall in her own deprivation and had volunteered at the homeless shelter in her free time. She bought her dad charming birthday gifts, and the homeless shelter made her a mobile saying she was wonderful, with each paper letter brightly colored, hanging from the stick. The "N" and "R" fell off in a week, so over her bed, for years, the stick slowly turned, announcing "WODEFUL." I am grateful, she'd said every day in high school, grateful for the food on my plate and the roof over my head. Grateful for my dad. Grateful I live in a country where we have options. For our beautiful environment, she said on Saturdays, sorting through the sticky plastic bottles at the recycling center.

Now, years later, even washing a single dish irritated her. I do everything around here, she grumbled to herself while moving the sponge over the circle. Even though she knew it wasn't true. She hadn't done the dishes in weeks. Daniel changed all the lightbulbs and paid the bills. He rubbed her feet and listened to her complaints. The truth was, she just didn't want to do anything at all. She did not want to have a job or have children or clean the bathroom or say hello. She only did a dish with happiness just after Daniel had done a dish. She only bought Daniel a present after he'd just bought a present for her, and even then she made sure her present wasn't quite as good as his.

It disgusted her as she did it, but it was the truth. She certainly liked the image of herself as the benevolent wife with arms full of flowers, but if she bought the flowers she would spend part of the ride home feeling so righteous and pleased that she had bought flowers; what a good wife she was; wasn't he a lucky man; until, by the time she arrived home with the flowers, she'd be angry he hadn't bought her flowers.

She reached out a hand to touch the cool sweep of the wall.

"It seems," she said to it, "that I have lost my generosity."

Her whole body filled with a sparkling panic, painful and visceral as poison champagne, because she did not know how to get it back.

The grand total on November 8 was $1,245. Daniel paid her the remaining money and gave her a fake sad look that could not disguise his relief, and then trundled off to the bathroom to get ready for work. She ironed the new bills, and packed them all into her tiny pocketbook of black velvet with the glittery clasp. The cash poked out its green fingers and her heels made pointed bites in the cement as she walked down the street, past the stores. She kept opening up the clasp of her purse and sticking her hand in there and stroking the money like it was a fur glove or a child's hair. What with the angle at which she held her bag and that look on her face, to passersby it seemed vaguely like she was masturbating.

People looked away. It was either that, or stare. She was magnetically disturbing to watch.

She stopped when she reached the mall, big and curvy. She roamed the three floors and mingled with all the people milling about with their big paper shopping bags and worn, drawn faces.

Inside the biggest and fanciest department store, at one end of the mall shops, she walked around the various sections of women's clothing, and observed all the different desks, and the different sets of salespeople. She watched for almost an hour, noting how each saleswoman interacted with customers, and how she looked, until she settled on the one she liked best. This was in the women's impulse department. The saleslady was about Janet's age, a little younger, and had a red velvet ribbon tied neatly around her neck, just like the horror story Janet had once heard about a woman who wears a velvet ribbon around her neck her whole life, every second of every day, until the one night when her curious husband removes it and her head falls off.

"Excuse me," said Janet, resting her pocketbook on the counter. "I have a question for you."

"Sure." The saleslady reupholstered her salesface in seconds. "How can I help you?"

"Do you support yourself?" Janet asked. She smiled, as amiably as she could.

"Pardon me?"

"I know it's an unusual question, but do you support yourself? Are you self-supported? Financially?"

The saleslady squinched up her nose. "Well," she said. "As a matter of fact, I am. Why do you ask?"

"And do you have a boyfriend?" Janet took in the bare left ring finger. Then she refixed her eyes on that red ribbon. The more she looked at it, the more it did seem to be glued to the woman's neck, and the red of the ribbon was the perfect shade to bring out the red in her lips and the brown of her eyes. It was the kind of glorious and simple fashion move you could stare at for hours in admiration.

The saleslady laughed, uncomfortable. "I'm sorry, are you looking for clothes, ma'am? These are fairly personal questions. There's a sale on pencil skirts on the right."

"But do you?"

"Why?"

"I'll look for clothes in a second," said Janet. "I need a cream turtleneck. Ribbed. Wool. Expensive. I'll need two, maybe three. But I'm just curious. Do you?"

"Well, yes," said the saleslady.

"Then, please, let me just ask you a little bit more," Janet said, leaning on the counter.

She hugged her pocketbook into her chest. "It's for a study. Who talks more?" she asked.

The saleslady narrowed her eyes at Janet, and then relaxed against the cash register. Business was slow; only a few other customers rotated around the perimeter of the department.

"You mean when? Like during dinner?" asked the saleslady.

"Whenever. Sure."

"Depends on who has more to say that day, I guess."

"And who pays, if you're out?"

"We usually split it," said the saleslady. "We both make about the same salary. Or one will take the other. There's no rule. What kind of turtleneck? You might want sportswear instead, that's one floor down. Did you say wool?"

Now, in addition to the ribbon, Janet noticed how the delicate mole punctuating the tip of the saleslady's eyebrow looked just like Venus at the tip of a crescent moon. Perfection.

"And do you regularly orgasm?" asked Janet.

"Excuse me?"

Janet held still. She could hear the cash registers erupt into sound around them.

Printing out receipts over the sounds of pens signing shiny credit card paper that curls into itself.

"Please," said Janet. "I know it's very forward, but please. It would mean an enormous amount to me to know."

The saleslady's eyes dodged around the store.

"The turtlenecks are downstairs," she said. "You'd better go down there. There's a woman downstairs in that department who likes to talk about things like this. You should ask her. Molly. Look for Molly."

Janet shook her head. "I want to ask you," she said.

The saleslady was fidgeting all around the cash register now, pushing buttons, ripping tissue paper, as if she were trapped in there.

Janet took a breath. "Look," she said. "I'm sure I seem crazy, but I'm not. I just don't know what it's like for other people. I live a sheltered life. Do you keep track? I don't want to ask Molly, because I don't want to be like Molly. This will be my last question, honestly."

Janet fumbled in her purse and pulled out two hundred-dollar bills.

"I'll pay you," she said firmly.

The saleslady stared at the bills and balled the ripped tissue paper into hard pellets.

"Two hundred dollars?" She glanced over her shoulder. "For one question? Are you serious?"

Janet didn't even blink.

The saleslady's eyebrows crunched in, and the mole pulled closer to her temple.

"It's for a study?"

A nod. "A self-study."

"And then you'll stop?"

Another nod.

"And are you a member of this store?"

Janet rummaged in her wallet and this time produced a bronze store credit card.

"Well," the saleslady said, bobbing her head tightly, "if it's worth that much to you. Fairly regularly, yes. What would you call regular?"

"Majority of the time," Janet said.

"Fine, then," said the saleslady. "Majority of the time. About seventy percent, through one method or another. Easier on some days than others. I don't keep track, no. Better off the pill than on. Nicer for me at night than in the morning. Now. Done! The turtlenecks are that way."

Her face was flushed. The red ribbon matched, in perfect harmony, the blush high on her cheeks.

Janet thrust the bills forward and held herself back from taking the woman's hand

37

and kissing it.

"Thank you." She felt her eyes watering. "You are really very beautiful." The yearning in her voice was so palpable it caught them both by surprise.

The saleslady stared at the money and broke into uncomfortable giggles before she grabbed it and strode off into the suit section. The older, blonder manager meandered over from across the room, sensing a need for managerial skills.

"Can I help you?" she asked Janet, now standing alone at the register.

"I need a turtleneck," said Janet.

In the horror story, the woman tells the man that she loves him, and she will marry him, but he must never remove the red velvet ribbon around her neck. It is the one thing he can never ask of her. At first it's the easiest trade; he complies for years and they are blissfully happy, but after a while it begins, in a slow broil, to burn him up inside. Why all the mystery? He unties the ribbon late at night, while she sleeps, and screams when her head rolls onto the floor.

Before, at summer camp, the story had always made Janet puff with righteousness. What a pushy spoiler of a husband. Wasn't their happiness enough? Couldn't he respect her one rule? One? But in the dressing room, her nose full of the clean smell of new turtleneck, she felt the story tugging at her. Something she couldn't quite put a finger on. As she paid cash for the turtle-necks — three: cream, fuchsia, black — she told a quick version of the story to the blonde manager, a woman who clearly knew her way in the world. Strong shoulders, proud large hands, open smile. "What do you think it means?" Janet asked. Far off in the distance, she could see the saleslady of her choice rehanging blouses on a rack.

The manager flattened out the receipt to sign.

"I remember that story," the manager said, sighing. "I had the cutest camp boy-friend."

"I mean, why not just be happy with the way things are, right?" said Janet.

The manager took the signed receipt and put it in the register's pile. She folded the turtlenecks, separating them with sheets of tissue paper, and then slipped all three into a bag. "But can you blame him?" she said, handing the bag to Janet. "I mean, I'm all for clothes, but at a certain point, they're supposed to go away, you know? How long were they married?"

"I don't know," said Janet, taking the bag.

"Story doesn't say."

"Take it all off!" said the manager. She winked at Janet. "Turtlenecks are good that way too."

Across the room, the woman with the red ribbon had finished lining up the blouses and moved on to the slacks. It was true, what the manager said. That ribbon was practically made to be removed. Even Janet herself wanted to slide over and undo the knot and unspool the choker from the woman's throat.

So — the man didn't know what was coming, Janet thought as she walked to the escalator. They'd been married for years, and he wanted her to give up the last thread of cover so she would stand before him nude and he could make love to her entire skin.

Well, of course that made her head fall off. Of course.

At home that night, wearing her new fuchsia turtleneck, Janet made a simple dinner of spaghetti and red sauce from a jar. She and Daniel ate together in silence. When they were both done, he cleared the dishes and put them in the sink.

"Thank you," he said, at the counter. "That was very good."

She watched him run water over the forks. His hair needed a cut — it was getting too long on the sides.

"It's November 9," he said.

"I know," she said. "Thank you again."

He dried the forks with a cloth. He seemed unusually quiet.

"You know, you were right," she said, brushing crumbs off the table into her palm. "What you said a few weeks ago. About your wife."

He didn't turn from the sink. "When I brought you flowers?"

"Yes."

"And what did I say again?"

"That she does not love you very well."

He ran his finger under the tap, back and forth, and poured a glob of dish soap on the pile of plates. "Actually, I think I said something different."

She picked up the drying cloth. "Oh?"

"I think I said that she doesn't love me at all."

He cleared a dish clean with the sponge.

She leaned over, to touch his arm. "Oh, Daniel," she said. "You know that's not true."

She could feel the turtleneck, climbing up to cover her neck, her shoulders, her torso. Pants, covering up her legs. Socks, over her

41

feet. Underwear, over her pubic hair. A bra, over her breasts.

"I want to do better," she said, quietly.

He placed a dish carefully in the dish rack, lining the circle up with the bent wire.

"Do you ever think about leaving?" he asked.

"No," she said.

He turned to her. His eyes were bright. "Sometimes I do," he said.

"Do what?"

"Think about leaving," he said.

She shook her head at him, confused. "But you can't leave," she said. "You're the devoted one."

His eyes were kind, and sad, at the sink.

"Are you leaving?" she said, and her voice rose, sharp.

"No." But there was a softness to his tone that implied a question, or the very first hint of a question mark, and she could see, suddenly, that they were on their way to leaving already, that this conversation was only a walking through a door already open, and once those eyes left they were not going to return and the clothing would be no barrier at all, nothing, shreds, tissue, for all the pain then rushing in.

TIGER MENDING

My sister got the job. She's the overachiever, and she went to med school for two years before she decided she wanted to be a gifted seamstress. (What? they said, on the day she left. A surgeon! they told her. You could be a tremendous surgeon! But she said she didn't like the late hours, she got too tired around midnight.) She has small motor skills better than a machine; she'll fix your handkerchief so well you can't even see the stitches, like she became one with the handkerchief. I once split my lip, jumping from the tree, and she sewed it up with ice and a needle she'd run through the fire. I barely even had a scar, just the thinnest white line.

So of course, when the two women came through the sewing school, they spotted her first. She was working on her final exam, a lime-colored ball gown with tiny diamonds sewn into the collar, and she was fully absorbed in it, constructing infinitesimal loops, while they hovered with their severe hair and heady tree-smell — like bamboo, my sister said — watching her work. My sister's so steady she didn't even flinch, but everyone else in class seized upon the distraction, staring at the two Amazonian women, both six feet tall and strikingly beautiful. When I met them later, I felt like I'd landed straight inside a magazine ad. At the time, I was working at Burger King, as block manager (there were two on the block), and I took any distraction offered me and used it to the hilt. Once, a guy came in and ordered a Big Mac, and for two days I told that story to every customer, and it's not a good story. There's so rarely any intrigue in this shabberdash world of burger warming; you take what you can get.

But my sister was born with supernatural focus, and the two women watched her and her alone. Who can compete? My sister's won all the contests she's ever been in, not because she's such an outrageous competitor, but because she's so focused in this gentle way. Why *not* win? Sometimes it's all you need to run the fastest, or to play the clearest piano, or to ace the standardized test, pausing at each question until it has slid through your mind to exit as a penciled-in circle.

In low, sweet voices, the women asked my sister if she'd like to see Asia. She finally looked up from her work. Is there a sewing job there? They nodded. She said she'd love to see Asia, she'd never left America. They said, Well, it's a highly unusual job. May I bring my sister? she asked. She's never traveled either.

The two women glanced at each other. What does your sister do?

She's manager of the Burger Kings down on Fourth.

Their disapproval was faint but palpable, especially in the upper lip.

She would simply keep you company?

What we are offering you is a position of tremendous privilege. Aren't you interested in hearing about it first?

My sister nodded lightly. It sounds very interesting, she said. But I cannot travel without my sister.

This is true. My sister, the one with that incredible focus, has a terrible fear of airplanes. Terrible. Incapacitating. The only way she can relax on a flight is if I am there, because I am always, always having some kind of crisis, and she focuses in and fixes me and forgets her own concerns. I become her ripped hemline. In general, I call her every night, and we talk for an hour, which is forty-five minutes of me, and fifteen minutes of her stirring her tea, which she steeps with the kind of Zen patience that would make Buddhists sit up in envy and then breathe through their envy and then move past their envy. I'm really really lucky she's my sister. Otherwise no one like her would give someone like me the time of day.

The two Amazonian women, lousy with confidence, with their ridiculous cheekbones, in these long yellow print dresses, said okay. They observed my sister's hands quiet in her lap.

Do you get along with animals? they asked, and she said, Yes. She loved every animal. Do you have allergies to cats? they asked, and she said, No. She was allergic only to pine nuts. The slightly taller one reached into her dress pocket, a pocket so well hidden inside the fabric it was like she was reaching into the ether of space, and from it her hand returned with an airplane ticket.

We are very happy to have found you, they said. The additional ticket will arrive tomorrow.

My sister smiled. I know her; she was probably terrified to see that ticket, and also she really wanted to return to the diamond loops. She probably wasn't even that curious about the new job yet. She was and is stubbornly, mind-numbingly, interested in the present moment.

When we were kids, I used to come home and she'd be at the living room window. It was the best window in the apartment, looking out, in the far distance, on the tip of a mountain. For years, I tried to get her to play with me, but she was unplayable. She stared out that window, never moving, for hours. By night, when she'd returned, I'd usually injured myself in some way or other, and I'd ask her about it while she tended to me; she said the reason she could pay acute attention now was because of the window. It empties me out, she said, which scared me. No, she said to my frightened face, as she sat on the edge of my bed and ran a washcloth over my forehead. It's good, she said. It makes room for other things.

Me? I asked, with hope, and she nodded. You.

We had no parents by that point. One had left, and the other died at the hands of a surgeon, which is the real reason my sister stopped medical school.

That night, she called me up and told me to quit my job, which was what I'd been praying for for months — that somehow I'd

47

get a magical phone call telling me to quit my job because I was going on an exciting vacation. I threw down my BK apron, packed, and prepared as long an account of my life complaints as I could. On the plane, I asked my sister what we were doing, what her job was, but she refolded her tray table and said nothing. Asia, I said. What country? She stared out the porthole. It was the pilot who told us, as we buckled our seat belts: we were heading to Kuala Lumpur, straight into the heart of Malaysia.

Wait, where's Malaysia again? I whispered, and my sister drew a map on the napkin beneath her ginger ale.

During the flight, I drank Bloody Marys while my sister embroidered a doily. Even the other passengers seemed soothed by watching her work. I whispered all my problems into her ear, and she returned them to me in slow sentences that did the work of a lullaby. My eyes grew heavy. During the descent, she gave the doily to the man across the aisle, worried about his ailing son, and the needlework was so elegant it made him feel better just to hold it. That's the thing with handmade items. They still have the person's mark on them, and when you hold them, you feel less alone. This is why everyone who eats a Whopper leaves a little more depressed than they were when they came in.

At the airport curbside, a friendly driver picked us up and took us to a cheerful green hotel, where we found a note on the bed telling my sister to be ready at 6 a.m. sharp. It didn't say I could come, but bright and early the next morning, scrubbed and fed, we faced the two Amazons in the lobby, who looked scornfully at me and my unsteady hands — I sort of pick at my hair a lot — and asked my sister why I was there. Can't she watch? she asked, and they said they weren't sure. She, they said, might be too anxious.

I swear I won't touch anything, I said.

This is a private operation, they said.

My sister breathed. I work best when she's nearby, she said. Please.

And like usual, it was the way she said it. In that gentle voice that had a back to it. They opened the car door.

Thank you, my sister said.

They blindfolded us for reasons of security, and we drove for more than an hour, down winding, screeching roads, parking finally in a place that smelled like garlic and fruit. In front of a stone mansion, two more women dressed in printed robes waved as we removed our blindfolds. These two were short. Delicate. Calm. They led us into the living room, and we hadn't been there for ten minutes when we heard the moaning.

A bad moaning sound. A real bad, real mournful moaning, coming from the north, outside, that reminded me of the worst loneliness, the worst long lonely night. The Amazonian with the short shining cap of hair nodded.

Those are the tigers, she said.

What tigers? I said.

Sssh, she said. I will call her Sloane, for no reason except that it's a good name for an intimidating person.

Sloane said, Sssh. Quiet, now. She took my sister by the shoulders and led her to the wide window that looked out on the land. As if she knew, instinctively, how wise it was to place my sister at a window.

Watch, Sloane whispered.

I stood behind. The two women from the front walked into view and settled on the ground near some clumps of ferns. They waited. They were very still-minded, like my sister, that stillness of mind. That ability I will never have, to sit still. That ability to have the hands forget they are hands. They closed their eyes, and the moaning I'd heard before got louder, and then, in the distance, I mean waaaay off, the moaning grew even

50

louder, almost unbearable to hear, and limping from the side lumbered two enormous tigers. Wailing as if they were dying. As they got closer, you could see that their backs were split open, sort of peeled, as if someone had torn them in two. The fur was matted, and the stripes hung loose, like packing tape ripped off their bodies. The women did not seem to move, but two glittering needles worked their way out of their knuckles, climbing up out of their hands, and one of the tigers stepped closer. I thought I'd lose it; he was easily four times the first woman's size, and she was small, a tiger's snack, but he limped over, in his giantness, and fell into her lap. Let his heavy striped head sink to the ground. She smoothed the stripe back over, and the moment she pierced his fur with the needle, those big cat eyes dripped over with tears.

It was very powerful. It brought me to tears, too. Those expert hands, as steady as if he were a pair of pants, while the tiger's enormous head hung to the ground. My sister didn't move, but I cried and cried, seeing the giant broken animal resting in the lap of the small precise woman. It is so often surprising, who rescues you at your lowest moment. When our father died in surgery, the jerk at the liquor store suddenly became the nicest man alive, and gave us free cranberry juice for a year.

What happened to them? I asked Sloane. Why are they like that?

She lifted her chin slightly. We do not know, but they emerge from the forests, peeling. More and more of them. Always torn at the central stripe.

Do they ever eat people?

Not so far, she said. But they do not respond well to fidgeting, she said, watching me clear out my thumbnail with my other thumbnail.

Well, I'm not doing it.

You have not been asked.

They are so sad, said my sister.

Well, wouldn't you be? said Sloane. If you were a tiger, unpeeling?

She put a hand on my sister's shoulder. When the mending was done, all four — women and beasts — sat in the sun for at least half an hour, tigers' chests heaving, women's hands clutched in their fur. The day grew warm. In the distance, the moaning began again, and two more tigers limped up while the first two stretched out and slept. The women sewed the next two, and the next. One had a bloody rip across its white belly.

After a few hours of work, the women put

their needles away, the tigers raised themselves up, and, without any lick or acknowledgment, walked off, deep into that place where tigers live. The women returned to the house. Inside, they smelled so deeply and earthily of cat that they were almost unrecognizable. They also seemed lighter, nearly giddy. It was lunchtime. They joined us at the table, where Sloane served an amazing soup of curry and prawns.

It is an honor, said Sloane, to mend the tigers.

I see, said my sister.

You will need very little training, since your skill level is already so high.

But my sister seemed frightened, in a way I hadn't seen before. She didn't eat much of her soup, and she returned her eyes to the window, to the tangles of fluttering leaves.

I would have to go find out, she said finally, when the chef entered with a tray of mango tartlets.

Find out what?

Why they unpeel, she said. She hung her head, as if she was ashamed of her interest.

You are a mender, said Sloane, gently. Not a zoologist.

I support my sister's interest in the source, I said.

Sloane flinched every time I opened my mouth.

The source, my sister echoed.

The world has changed, said Sloane, passing a mango tartlet to me, reluctantly, which I ate, pronto.

It was unlike my sister to need the cause. She was fine, usually, with just how things were. But she whispered to me — as we roamed outside looking for clues, of which we found none — she whispered that she felt something dangerous in the unpeeling, and she felt she would have to know about it in order to sew the tiger suitably. I am not worried about the sewing, she said. I am worried about the gesture I place inside the thread.

I nodded. I am a good fighter, is all. I don't care about thread gestures, but I am willing to throw a punch at some tiger asshole if need be.

We spent the rest of the day outside, but there were no tigers to be seen — where they lived was somewhere far, far off, and the journey they took to arrive here must have been the worst time of their lives, ripped open like that, suddenly prey to vultures or other predators, when they were usually the ones to instill fear.

We slept that night at the mansion, in

feather beds so soft I found them impossible to sleep in. Come morning, Sloane had my sister join the two women outside, and I cried again, watching the big tiger head at her feet while she sewed with her usual stillness. The three together were unusually productive, and sewn tigers piled up around them. But instead of that giddiness that showed up in the other women, my sister grew heavier that afternoon, and said she was sure she was doing something wrong. Oh no, said Sloane, serving us tea. You were remarkable.

I am missing something, said my sister. I am missing something important.

Sloane retired for a nap, but I snuck out. I had been warned, but really, they were treating me like shit anyway. I walked a long distance, but I'm a sturdy walker, and I trusted where my feet went, and I did not like the sight of my sister staring into her teacup. I did not like the feeling it gave me, of worrying. Before I left, I sat her in front of the window and told her to empty herself, and her eyes were grateful in a way I was used to feeling in my own face but was not accustomed to seeing in hers.

I walked for hours, and the wet air clung to my shirt and hair. I took a nap inside some ferns. The sun was setting, and I would've walked all night, but when I reached a cluster of trees, something felt different. There was no wailing yet, but I could feel the stirring before the wailing, which is almost worse. I swear I could hear the dread. I climbed up a tree and waited.

I don't know what I expected — people, I guess. People with knives, cutting in. I did not expect to see the tigers themselves, jumpy, agitated, yawning their mouths beyond wide, the wildness in their eyes, and finally the yawning so large and insistent that they split their own backs in two. They all did it, one after another — as if they wanted to pull the fur off their backs, and then, amazed at what they'd done, the wailing began.

One by one, they left the trees and began their slow journey to be mended. It left me with the oddest, most unsettled feeling.

I walked back when it was night, under a half-moon, and found my sister still at the window.

They do it to themselves, I whispered to her, and she took my hand. Her face lightened. Thank you, she said. She tried to hug me, but I pulled away. No, I said, and in the morning, I left for the airport.

FACES

On an unusual day during my childhood, my mother showed up at school and asked me questions about myself. I was twelve or so then, and generally I found my own way home: bus, walk, hitchhike, bike, get pushed forward by the shoe soles of others. I hardly recognized her car, waiting there by the flagpole with all the other mothercars until she honked and beckoned me inside.

"I'm not supposed to talk to strangers," I said at the window.

"Get in, William," she said, pushing open the door. "How was school?"

"Why are you picking me up?"

"Get *in*," she said, pushing the door open more.

I had, right then, a fast stab of fear in my stomach, like maybe she would kidnap me. Except for the fact that she had birthed me. It was confusing.

I settled into the passenger seat.

"So," she said, as she pulled out of the school lot. "How was your day?"

"Fine," I said.

"How are your friends?"

"Fine," I said.

"That's good. What did you do today?"

"We played war. How are you?"

. . .

. . .

"You played war on the playground?"

"Yes."

"War is not a game, William. Your uncle —"

"I mean we played tag. I forgot. Sorry."

"Oh. And was that fun?"

"Sure."

"I've always enjoyed tag myself."

"Tag is a classic."

We turned onto the main street, by the shopping area. My mother used to work nearby as an administrative assistant, but she had lost her job the month before. "We have nothing left to administer," they told her.

"And who do you like the best of your friends?" she said.

"Mom," I asked, picking at the seat belt, "why are you here? It smells like French fries."

"Is there a friend you like more than the

others?"

"Not really," I said. "I like them all the same."

She eyed the driver behind us in her rearview mirror, waving as she changed lanes.

"Where are we going?" I asked.

"Nowhere special. Do you have someplace to be?"

"Me?"

"Yes."

"Do I have someplace to be?"

"Yes."

"No."

"Good, then. Now, why don't you tell me one of your friends' names."

"Why are you so interested all of a sudden?"

"I just want to know one of your friends' names," she said, slowing down at a light.

"Gath," I said.

"Last name?"

"Gath."

"First name?"

"Gath."

"Gath Gath?"

"Sure."

She smiled straight ahead, but her eyes were wavering.

"What do you mean, *sure*?"

"That sounds about right," I said. "Can we stop for fries?"

"But is it his real name?"

"I don't know."

"You don't know?"

"Gath Gath?"

"Sounds good to me," I said.

"You don't know your friends' names?"

I opened the glove box to discover many neat stacks of paper about cars and their insides.

"So what do you call them if their back is to you?"

I thought about it for a second. The car in front of us had a kid facing out in the backseat, waving and waving.

"I call them Hey or You," I said, waving back.

She almost laughed, but it turned into a grunt. The kid turned left. Bye. We drove into the mall, and I sat in the parking lot while she went shoe shopping. Half an hour later, she returned, smelling suspiciously of chocolate cake. "The shoes in there," she said, "are so expensive!" She handed over a bread roll. She didn't want to bring me in with her because last time mall security found me quietly moving items in the department store into the wrong departments.

■ ■ ■ ■

She brought it all up again at the dinner table that night, over spaghetti and red sauce.

"My friends have many names," said my little sister, Ginny, promptly. "Angie, Kevette, Marjorie, Orrel —"

"Shut up," I said. "Eat your dinner."

Dad tilted his head down to his plate. He wasn't often home before nine, so this was a rare encounter, to be all eating at the same time. It felt like some kind of grand coincidence.

"What's the problem?" he asked.

My mother shook her head. "You don't get it," she said. "He honestly doesn't know his friends' *names,* and these are kids he sees at school every single day."

"I know who they are," I said. "They're my group of friends."

"Do they look different to you?" she asked.

"What do you mean?"

"I mean can you tell them apart from each other?"

I took a sip of juice to stall. "What do you mean?"

"I mean — do you know one from the other?"

"Three of them are kind of the same," I said, wiping my mouth. "Then there's the really tall one! He's different."

My mother stared at my father. "Are you hearing this?"

"I'm exhausted," he said, drawing his hand down his face. "I think I single-handedly saved the company today."

"Which company?" asked Ginny.

"The one that sells bottles," he said. "The plastic-bottle one."

"Oh!" she said. "My favorite!" She jumped down from her chair and sped into the bathroom, then returned with a yellow plastic bottle of shampoo, just to show she could identify his work in the world at large. He mussed her hair. My mother poured herself a little glass of cheap sherry and forwent her spaghetti altogether, and who can blame her, since it was pretty much just noodles stirred with ketchup.

"So," said my mother. "You can't tell your friends from each other. Can you tell me from your father?"

"Sure, Dad," I said. "Easy."

She coughed mid-sip. Dad was explaining plastic-bottle structure to Ginny and didn't hear, which is too bad, because he, for one, might've laughed.

"Am I Mom?" asked Ginny, pretending to

listen to Dad.

"Your uncles," asked Mom.

"I've never met," I said.

"Your grandparents?"

"Which ones?"

"Any."

"I can mostly tell them apart," I said. "For example, there's the demented one."

"William!" said my mother, clearing her dish. She scraped spaghetti into the trash can.

"There is a lipid in the cellular structure," said Dad.

"We need to take you to the doctor," Mom said. "There's something very wrong with you."

"He is so messed up," murmured Ginny.

"Why'd you pick me up today in the first place?" I asked.

My mother sipped her sherry in the kitchen and sniffed. My father had evaporated from the table by now; I found him reconstituted on the sofa, asleep, with a book on his lap about the history of plastics, and the bottle of shampoo nestled against his stomach like a baby.

The next day, my relentless mother:

"Enough kidding around, William," she said. "You're very funny. Now, who, specifically, did you eat lunch with today?"

"All five Gath brothers," I said. "They were at school two days in a row!"

"And which one is the nicest?" she asked.

"None of them is the least bit nice."

She stopped dusting a birdbath made of wire, complete with wire birds and little wire-looped water drops falling from a wire tree.

"Or which Gath brother talks the most?"

"All of them the same."

"No one talks more than the others?"

"No," I said. "All of them at once."

"How can you possibly understand anything if they're all talking at once?"

"Easy," I said, swaying. "You just go with the flow of it."

She shook her rag in the air, and a muggy cloud of dust sank to the carpet. "This is rapidly becoming like a bad Abbott and Hardy routine," she said. "Except it isn't funny."

"Why are you so interested all of a sudden?" I said. "Who are *your* friends? How come I don't know any of their names?"

She closed the shelf and locked it, half-dusted. She always locked it, like I was going to steal a wire birdbath and keep it for my very own. Then she brought out a series of knickknacks and put them on the coffee table. A stone lizard, an ashtray of rock, a glass princess.

"Never mind me," she said. "Now, which one is glass?"

I pointed to the princess. "I'm not stupid," I said.

"Which one is a lizard?"

I pointed to the ashtray.

"The lizard, William," she said.

I pointed at the ashtray again, with no expression.

She blinked up at me, alarmed, and I held it for a second and then just laughed and laughed until I fell on the floor, laughing. I had to eat dinner that night in my room. Leftover ketchup spaghetti, cold. I have no problem at all identifying objects.

Later that night, when I took out the trash, I found a magazine called *Mother Magazine* on top of the pile, and to make my sleuthing even easier, it fell right open to a quiz called "How Well Do You Know Your Children?" I could see her fresh pencil scrawls all over the page. Questions like: *Do you know where your child is after school?* She had G: "yes." W: "no." *Do you know the names of your child's friends?* G: "yes." W: "no." *Do you know your child's favorite color?* G: "yellow." W: "blue." (Which is wrong. I don't believe in picking a favorite color; it seems like a pretty dumb thing to rank, if you ask me.) *Do you know any of your child's fears?* G: "death, and chemical warfare." W: "?Friends?" And: *Do you know what your child might like to be when he/she grows up?* G: "vet or singer." W: "?army?"

The magazine had a rating scale too — if you got 85–100 percent of the questions, which she did with Ginny, you were "A Mother to Be Reckoned With!" and it said how great you were, how tuned in, how involved. The middle category was something like "Hang In There, Mom, You're Trying!" and the final one, which she got for me, was "Mother, May I Suggest Some Mothering?"

"This was all for a *quiz*?" I said to her when I went inside, washing trash juice off my hands, and she finished folding up the newspaper into neat rectangles and said she was sure she had no idea what I was talking about.

The following day, after school, we drove half an hour away to the doctor, who was both a specialist in perception and also miraculously covered under our scant insurance. In the waiting room, we sat on different sofas, and my mother read the magazine on brides and I read the one with the weekly news report that has a section in the back about how to raise your kid, which I find hilarious.

"Robertson!" called out the receptionist. I grabbed a handful of hard candies on my way in.

The doctor's chambers were white-walled and blue-trash-canned and orange-chaired. I ate a cinnamon and a peppermint at once. The doctor strode in with coat and clipboard, and my mother launched into it right away: "Hello there, Doctor, thank you so much for seeing us, my son has this funny thing where he has trouble telling the difference between a group and a person."

"Well," chortled the doctor, "isn't that interesting."

Her neck was so long it seemed strange that she was a doctor specializing in perception.

"Let's see what we can discover here," she said. "Hi, William."

"Hi."

She stuck instruments into my eyes. She made me read various letters across the room. She had me close one eye and then the other.

"His vision is fine," she said, after ten minutes.

"Ah," said my mother.

I chomped down on a butterscotch, and a little shard of gold sugar flew up and stuck on the doctor's white coat collar.

"Sorry," I said.

She brushed off her coat and put a few slides up on the wall and had me explain them: Does the line appear to be wavy? It's really straight. Does the circle above appear to be smaller? It's really the same size as the one below. "But doesn't everyone have these perception problems?" I asked, after identifying both the witch and the young girl in the same drawing of a face. "True," she said. "Sure. But they're fun to look at, aren't they?"

She turned the slide projector off and rummaged in a drawer, returning with a photograph of a group of people.

"Let's try this," she said. "William, who are these people?"

"They're a group of people," I said.

She bobbed her head. "Mmm-hmmm. Okay. And what do these people do?"

"They're all nurses," I said.

"That's right!"

I pointed to the bottom of the photo, where it said *Nurse Convention* on a black plaque in big white letters.

She nodded; her neck was so long that a nod for her took about four seconds to complete.

"And what can you tell me about any of the people in the picture?"

"They're all nurses," I said again.

"And how are they different?"

"They're different heights," I said.

"Okay." She looked in my ear while I was talking.

"My ears feel fine," I said.

"She's checking your balance," whispered my mother, sitting perfectly still in a stiff orange chair in the corner.

The doctor straightened the photo in front of me.

"Now, William," she said, "can you tell me if any of the nurses are older than the others?"

"What do you mean?"

"I mean, are there elderly nurses in the photo?"

I peered at it. They all looked pretty old to me. I found one with white hair.

"This one seems old," I said. "He has white hair."

She looked over my shoulder at the photo. "Okay," she said. "Good. And you can tell that it's a man there."

"Yes," I said. "It's an old man nurse, right there."

"And what else can you tell me about them?"

"Nothing much," I said. "A bunch of nurses in a photo. For a convention."

She returned to the drawer and brought out another picture. The second photo was of a bunch of young men in the army.

"Soldiers," I said, pleased with myself. I could tell from the camouflage clothing.

"Okay," she said. "And?"

"And what?"

"And . . . how are they different?"

"What do you mean?" I asked. "From each other? They're all soldiers."

"For example," she said, "are some happy?"

I looked at it again. They were moving around, some of them. "Sure," I said. "I suppose some are."

"Can you tell?"

"Not really," I said. "You can't ever tell for sure if someone's happy or not."

She pointed to the corner with her fingertip. "What about this one here?"

"What about him?"

"How is he doing?"

I peered closely at his face. "I don't think he looks too good," I said. "His expression is weird."

The doctor blew her nose into a tissue.

"He's getting shot," she said.

"Oh," I said. "Huh. I didn't see that part yet."

"You didn't see his torso?"

"No," I said. "I was looking at his face, like you asked. Now that I look at his body, I can see that he is getting shot."

"And so is he happy?"

"Well, I certainly doubt it," I said. "I'm not a moron."

"And are any of them dead?"

I looked again at the photo. It took me a long time. Several of the soldiers were lying down. One of the ones lying down had his face in the dirt.

"This one could be dead," I said, after about five minutes. "But maybe he's sleeping."

She unscrewed the earpiece from her instrument and took the photo out of my hands. "Thank you, William," she said. "Fine. Let's take a break and try something else for a minute. Of your friends at school, whom do you like the best?"

I could actually hear my mother's jaw stiffen behind me.

"I like them the same," I said.

"Really?" she asked.

"Really."

"And do you have friends at school?"

"I just said so, didn't I? I have a couple of groups I float between; I'm not really in one main group."

"And can you tell the two groups from each other?"

"Of course," I said, ripping up the corner of the papery doctor-visit shirt.

"How?"

"They sit in different parts of school," I said.

"I see," said the doctor. "And is there a leader in these groups?"

"They change around," I said.

I turned and glared at my mother. She had her head down, her eyes on the wall, the ceiling, the floor.

"Can we move on, Doc?" I asked. "Any more photos?"

The doctor wrote something on her clipboard and returned to the drawer to take out another picture, this one of a family. I wasn't sure why she had all these group pictures in her drawer, but maybe she saw people like me all the time.

"How about them?" she asked.

"Yes?"

"What can you tell me about them?"

"They're all black," I said. "I can see that."

"Can you pick out the grandfather?"

I looked for a while. No one had white

72

hair. "No."

"Can you pick out the baby?"

I looked for a while again, and finally I found a baby stroller, off in the corner.

"There," I said. "A baby."

"Can you find the young man?"

I stared at it, but I couldn't find the young man any more than I could tell who was the grandfather. And just because someone was old didn't mean he was a grandfather anyway.

"No," I said. "And it's not because I'm racist."

She brought out a similar photo of a family of white people. All I got was the shape of the group made by their heights and the positions of arms and feet.

"This one is sitting," I said, pointing.

The doctor looked at my mother now. They exchanged a meaningful look.

"What?" I said. "Do I have brain damage? What? Who cares who's who? I enjoy the general. What's so wrong with that? Why is this important? If I meet the person and talk to them, I'll know who they are then."

My mother was silent.

The doctor was silent.

"Why did you say that?" asked the doctor, after a minute.

"What do you mean?"

"Why did you just say all that?"

"Because I hate snap judgments," I said.

The doctor folded her arms.

"But how do you know?" she asked.

"How do I know what?"

"How do you know we're making snap judgments?"

I unwrapped another candy. Green peppermint. "No reason," I said. "My mother gave you a look."

Now the doctor leaned against the wall.

"So you could see her look?"

"What do you mean?" I asked. "Didn't she give you a look?"

"Yes," Mom said. "I gave her a look."

"But you could *see* your mother's look," said the doctor. "Why?"

"Why?"

"You can't see an old man. You can't see a soldier getting shot."

"I know my mother's face."

"Can you see it now?"

I looked over. Truth was, I couldn't really see her face. I could see big red lips because she was wearing lipstick because she likes to look nice for doctors.

"Make a face, Mrs. Robertson," the doctor said.

She did something. What, I couldn't tell.

"Can't tell," I said, sucking on the candy.

"But you could tell the earlier look," said the doctor.

"Just sometimes," I said. "Are we done?"

"Do you see me as a group?" asked the doctor then, in an all-too-friendlyvoice.

"I am not retarded," I said, pulling my shirt back over my head. "I can see that you are one person, and that you have a ridiculously long neck."

"William!" barked my mother.

"William, may I speak to your mother alone for a moment?" the doctor asked.

I stormed out. I emptied the entire lobby candy jar into my pockets and left the building. There was a candle shop next door, so I went in there and smelled wax for a while; the one that said it smelled like chocolate was wildly misleading. I have an excellent sense of smell. On the street, I tried to look at all the people walking by, but they just looked like walking people to me. I didn't see why I needed to read their faces. Wasn't there enough complication in the world already without having to take in the overload of details and universes in every single person's fucking face?

The drive home was mostly silent. My mother didn't wave at the drivers when she changed lanes, which is unlike her. In general, she's at her best in the world with strangers, and gets great reassurance from a wave or a nod between cars. But on this drive home she changed lanes on her own without acknowledgment of anyone and was quiet until we pulled into the driveway.

"I just don't understand," is all she said then.

My dad walked in from work late that night, as usual, and found some frozen pizza thawing in the refrigerator by accident. It had never been cooked, but he didn't bother to heat it up and just ate it cold. "Cold pizza," he said, smiling at me, as little flecks of cheese fell to the floor. "It's not the same," I told him. When he was done, my mother asked if she could speak to him in the other room. Ginny was playing hospital with her torn stuffed animals, and I skulked around their door as they settled in the bedroom and I heard her whisper to my dad that we went today to the doctor who did lots of tests and was very kind and professional and William has a real problem and the doctor diagnosed him with facial illiteracy.

"Wait, what?" I said from the hallway. I leaned in the door frame. "She said what?"

My mother's eyes were enormous. Okay, I could see them. My mom only, sometimes.

My father's hair was a mess from exhaustive mussing, and he said: "Facial illiteracy? What the hell is that?"

"He cannot read a face," said my mother, wincing. "He cannot recognize facial or, for that matter, bodily signals. He can't read people at all. And, Stan," she said, "it's true."

"Oh, what*ever,*" I said, kicking the door. "I bet the doctor made that name up right on the spot."

"Go to bed, William."

"It's nine o'clock."

"You're a growing boy. Go to bed."

"So what does it mean?" asked my father.

"I don't know," she said. "He may have to take special classes. On recognition. Of faces and people. *Go to bed,* William!"

I stayed by the door until she came and closed it on me.

Shoving my ear against the wood, I heard my father's tones of mild protest and my mother's rising pierce. "Soldiers!" she was saying. "All dead! He thought they were happy!"

At the TV, I found Ginny surrounded by her now mended stuffed toys, watching the sitcom about the people who work at the pet store and act like animals. She likes the boss, who talks like a monkey. I tried to look at each actor's individual face, but all I saw were eyebrows and teeth. No one emerged from the parental bedroom for over an hour, and I fell asleep on the couch. That's where I woke up with the first light of morning, covered with stuffed bears just barely held together by clusters of staples and tape.

(There was a moment, once. I was eating dinner with Mom, and Dad was at work late, and Ginny was at a friend's house learning fractions. I barely remember this; it's sort of made up, if you want to know the truth. But we were eating spaghetti and cottage cheese, and Mom looked at me, and then all of sudden it was like her face melted; the lines around her eyes all pointed down, arrows down her face to the lines around her mouth, which pointed down, and then her chin caught it all like a net, trapping all the down arrows and feeding them back into her jaw and lower lip, which drooped and sank from the weight.

She took a sip of her water.

"Mom, you okay?" I asked.

"Sure," she said. "Why?")

For about a month, I went to classes across town taught by the long-necked doctor.

78

They involved me and her in a dark viewing room, looking at huge slides of babies' faces crying and laughing, and I had to tell her which was which. The doctor was stupid, because she kept using the same set of slides, and each time she'd tell me which was which, not realizing that every slide had a small gold number embossed in the corner. I just made notes on my leg: 14 is laughing, 13 is sneezing, 12 is crying, 11 is sleeping, etc. Within two weeks, I got eight out of ten on the test (I missed two on purpose), and she seemed very pleased with both of us. "Let's see how you do for now," she said, and she let me have my Saturday mornings back, which I used to climb roofs and mess with people's TV antennae.

(I was walking to school with Ginny. She was telling me about her verb project, where she is gathering under-appreciated verbs, and putting them to use. "Look, I'm sauntering to school," she said, doing a little trick with her feet. She tilted her head to the side for a second, and she's a few years younger than me, and when she squinted, putting her lips to one side, for a second I thought she looked hot. I'm making this up. She's nine. She crossed the street and yelled, "Behold you later!" over her shoulder.)

My mother did not pick me up from school again. She was back pounding the streets, looking for a job. She did interrogate me several times at the kitchen table when we were home at the same time, but by now I'd learned my lesson. "His name's John Gath," I said to her, as I ate my fifth piece of toast. "He talks the most of anyone, and he is the leader of the group. I like him the best, except on the days when he's in a bad mood."

"John?" she said.

"John," I said, chewing the crust. "And his brothers are George and Paul, and his cousins are Rocky and Jo-Jo."

"And who talks the least?" she asked, brushing ants into the trash can. I watched them climb out.

"Jo-Jo," I said, "is a quiet sort. By the way, my favorite color is blue."

"Blue," she sighed, leaning back on the counter. "That's a good one. Have you done your homework?"

"All done," I said. "Did you get a job?"

"Soon," she said.

(We were smoking at the wall at recess,

and one of the Gaths handed me a bag of barbecue chips, and when I took it, he had this look in his eye. Glinty. Looking right at me. "What?" I said. "What?" he said.)

You know what I like to look at? The birdbaths, locked up. The stuffed bear stuck together with staples and tape. The TV. The refrigerator. I like the car. The changing weather. The taste of wrong-color peppermints. The doctor's neck.

(There's a photo of the Robertson family in a blue wooden frame that sits on top of the TV that we got done at the department store's photo department. I try to focus my attention on the TV, but sometimes I glance up by accident. Mostly I just see hair and all of us in our nice shirts and I remember the dick photographer who made us say "buttercream pie," but once in a while, I look up and it's a flash, like the photograph is screaming and everything is imprinted there, everything. Like the shape of my mother's jaw might as well bleed out the word "disappointment" and my dad's eyes are way far back and blank in his head and Ginny smiles too big like she's

pouring grout on the world and some-
body's flattened me.

One night, Mom held it up during
commercials and said, "I think this is
my favorite picture of us yet," because
she likes how the angle doesn't show her
double chin and she likes to see Ginny
smiling with her pretty teeth and Dad
with his hair just cut, and how for once
I wasn't scowling at the camera.

"Look, William, how handsome you
are when you're not being difficult," she
said.

I shrugged at her. "Can't see it," I said.
"Sorry.")

ON A SATURDAY AFTERNOON

I have known them for at least three years, these two; we all went to school together, and at one point I dated the blond but it was brief. The timing was off and both of us were swept along by the river of another match. I have flirted with the brown-haired one for years.

I have this fantasy, I say one evening, when all of us are slightly drunk, sitting on my apartment steps on Gardner on a clear July night. Would you come back? Four o'clock? Saturday?

Sure, they tell me, curious. The word marked by brake lights and bitten fingernails. Everybody facing out. We all hold hands at once, and we are all lonely when we go home, but this is helpful, this handholding, this sitting on the stoop of my apartment building, watching while other people look for parking.

I have recently broken up with someone

whom I did not expect to break up with, and every morning, the earliest time I wake up is suffused with remembering; I can't seem to beat that moment, no matter how early I rise. I once thought if I traveled in France I would have a different brain, the brain of a girl who travels in France. I saw myself, skipping through meadows in a yellow-and-blue-print dress. But even with the old buildings, with the bright bready smells, with the painted French sunlight, it was still my same brain in there, chomping as usual, just fed this time by baguettes and Brie.

In the mornings I write long circular journal entries when I wake up. Too early. Before work. But even though I am making steady proclamations about who I will go for next, and why, and how it will all be different, it is brutal to imagine the idea of meeting a new person. Going through the same routine. Saying the same phrases I have now said many times: the big statements, the grand revelations about my childhood and character. The cautious revealings of insecurities. I have said them already, and they sit in the minds of those people who are out living lives I have no access to anymore. A while ago, this sharing was tremendous; now the idea of facing a new person and speaking the same core sentences seems like a mistake, an error of integrity. Surely it is not good for my own mind to make myself into a speech like that. The only major untouched field of discussion will have to do with this feeling, this tiredness, this exact speech.

The next person I love, I will sit across from in silence. We will have to learn it from each other some other way.

On Saturday, there's a knock at the door right at four, and I open it up. Hi! Hi, hi. We're all joking and nervous, and they brought beer. Me too. I usher them in. My apartment sometimes reminds people of a warehouse; the space is high and elongated and feels empty. The living room is a stripe. It's too narrow to watch TV in, so I put the furniture on a diagonal.

They both look great, thriving out of control. These are solid men, with square kneecaps and loving mothers, who are still sort of awed by women. They have a line of fur instead of hair at the napes of their necks, sometimes dusting the hinge of their cleanly shaven jaws. Me, I'm clothed and workmanlike in overalls with many pockets. A red tank top, legs covered. They have had crushes on me at some point, and me on them, but everyone knew that friendship was best, and it is in this spirit that they walk through my door. They're good at the greeting hug routine. There is a wild fondness in the air. We grab beers, twist off, fling bottle caps into the air.

They're friends with each other, too. Sometimes they play soccer together.

They said they would do what I asked them to. That's the agreement. It's a four o'clock afternoon and the July sun is lazy and inviting and it's a second-floor apartment, so it's always a little warm from the rising heat, and here are these two men I've captured, inside my house, wearing worn white T-shirts. One of them has a stain right in the middle from the peach cobbler he ate at lunch, left over from the potluck he went to Friday night at Valerie's. He is the type everyone gives their leftovers to at the end of the party, because they know he will eat them, and he does. Somehow this makes me proud. Whenever these two walk down hallways, or through crosswalks, in their tall boyishness I feel a surge of pride that is faintly motherly and also not. I want to fuck and birth them at the same time.

Today, they have another beer. Me too. We joke around. We play bottle-cap hockey. I serve cookies on a chipped green plate.

They eat them, fast. They have sweet tooths, they say. One prefers the chocolate chip; the other enjoys the texture of oatmeal. They're deep in the stripe, by the windows at its end, and I sit down in the chair that I've placed closer to the door. Stay over there, I tell them, as they swallow the last two bites off the plate. All right, they say. They sprawl out on the carpet, hands propping up their heads, and they know how to own space, how to feel important without realizing it. They have never questioned their right to be alive; it is borne in them, and obvious. One is wearing shorts and has blond hair all over his pale knees. Like poured milk from a glass carton.

Okay, I say, after the third beer is finished. I bring out tequila. I give each of us two shots. Down, down, down.

Then: Just touch hands, I say.

One touches his own hands. No, I say. His. His hand. Touch that.

It takes until just now for them to realize I want them to touch each other. They have assumed they'll be touching me. I don't have shoes on, but I have the rest on, and maybe a ponytail. I'm in the day. Just touch hands, I say. Gently. Please. They look bewildered — not upset, just unsure. They will need my constant reassurance. This is why I will not feel left out.

It's okay, I tell them. Just feel his arm. Maybe the back of his neck. Just see what it feels like.

The sun slants through the curtains as their two hands reach over and they sort of grab at first but then relax. They explore the knuckles, the wrists, the elbows. They don't giggle, but there is some nervous shifting, some more drinking from beers. Wet barley lips. One is from Oklahoma, and came out west to direct movies. The other lived in Oregon, in a clapboard house with an attic where he gathered bird nests from trees. They remember their first kiss with a girl, the years of masturbating in the shower before their sisters would bang on the door, yelling about hot water.

They are touching each other's arms now, with freckles, with downy hair. Touch his stomach, I say, to both. Four eyes beam up at me, frightened. It's okay, I say. It's for me, I say. Please. And their hands, shaking slightly, reach down under the loose T-shirts and just glance over their stomachs, which have tiny lines of sweat forming in the creases from sitting.

I am in my chair. They feel scared, even from over here, but not awful scared. They're openhearted and they can stand it.

They have untested liberal minds. They are also getting turned on. Their faces move closer together as one grazes the inner arm of the other.

Kiss him, I say, out loud.

The light through the drawn curtains is a dark red and partially obscures their clean-shaven faces. They lean in, and their cheeks bump at first and finally touch. Their lips, so soft. They are tentative and frightened, faces pressing gently against each other. Lips meet. Boy lips on boy lips. I love watching them. I could watch them for hours. Their heads leaning and listing, the lips learning what to do, how almost-familiar it all is.

One stops. Looks at me. Is this all right? he asks. His lips glisten. Why don't you come join us —

I'm watching this time, I say. Just watching. You're so beautiful, both of you.

The other turns to me, eyes overly bright-ened. Come on, he calls. Come over!

I shake my head.

Absolutely! they both say.

No.

I'm on the weird island, over here. They love me too; I'm not totally absented. We all know I'm in the room.

Keep kissing, I say. I can't tell you how

much I love to watch you kissing.

Their big young male faces drink more beer and then lean back in and I see the erections, poking up from their pants, and they seem hopeful and nervous and vulnerable, and as they keep kissing, hands moving now down shoulders, to back, to stomach, I tell them to take off their shirts, and they do, because today they listen to me. I will not hurt them. I can only get away with this once. And the shoes kick off, and the pants roll down, and there they are, nude and strong, poking each other in the stomach. More beer. More tequila. Eyes closed. The reddish light flutters on the floor, and cars honk downstairs. I tell the one on the right, the one with the brown curls in his hair, to lean down. To try it out. Please, I say again. Please. My voice is so quiet, but we all hear everything. He bends down. The one on his knees now has on his face a combination of pained concern or confusion over what this might mean and utter joy too, and he opens his eyes and glances at me, and I smile at him, my whole body awake. He can see how turned on I am. There's a furrow of worry in his brow, so I reach to the overalls straps and unclip them and pull my shirt up so that there are breasts in the room. Visiting. His face lights up, in part because he likes them, but even more because he knows them, he recognizes the shape, they are a marking point for identity and memory.

And then my overalls are back on and he closes his eyes again, I have relieved some knot in his thinking, and the first one is curled over and he doesn't know quite what to do but also he has some ideas, and his mouth is earnest and effortful.

Their hands grip the carpet hairs. Look at the initial swell of a bicep, that bump after the dip of the inner elbow.

When they switch, they're laughing. Everyone's drunk. No one has come yet. They kiss in between switching, and their hands move all over, into inner thigh, rounded curve of the ass, sweaty necks. I feel the tide fading from my feet. They look up — come with us, come join us, they say, but I'm over here, I say, for today — and at once they are disappointed and also we all know the rhythm has been set as is. Tight calves and legs lifting. Brown curls and blond knees. When they're kissing again, I could stare for hours. Men love to watch two women kiss, but how I love to watch two men. So clear in their focus. The amazing space created for me when there is nothing demanded or seen.

■ ■ ■ ■

When they are sleeping, I go into my bedroom. It is darker than the rest of the apartment, and only large enough to fit a bed and a dresser. I don't sit down, but I stand with the furniture, my whole body triggered. And it is only now that I feel the coldness of watching, the interminable loneliness, how the exit will happen, how they will hug me but something will have shifted, how our meetings will be awkward for a while, and possibly never recover. I slow down my breathing, move away from the clawing inside. After a while, I hear as they get up off the floor and let themselves out. They leave me a nice note, and one washes the cookie dish, and they even put the beer bottles in the recycling bin, but the rest of the evening is nothing but the trembling edges of something I am so tired of feeling and do not want to feel anymore.

PART TWO

THE FAKE NAZI

1.

There was an old man in Germany who thought he was a Nazi. He turned himself in to a small court in a town near Nuremberg, and said, "Restart the trials; I should be punished for what I have done." He seemed to be around the right age, and his name was a fairly common German name — Hoefler — and his first name even more common — Hans — but still, they had records and looked up as many Hans Hoeflers as they could and cross-referenced and found nothing. "Where were you?" they asked him repeatedly. He lowered his eyes. "I was in the room for all of it," he told them. "What room?" they asked. "The ROOM," he said. They raised their eyebrows. "Of which room are you speaking?" they said. "There were many."

"I heard the planning," he said. "I popped the Zyklon B. I shot rows and rows of people."

The judge coughed into his fist. Hans broke down crying, begging for forgiveness, and the secretary found herself resisting the urge to pat him on the head, which seemed like the wrong idea altogether. They found a photo of him at the time, sitting with small children in the park as a babysitter for the neighbors; turned out he was then only a child himself, and would never have been allowed in any "room" anyway. He was an old man by the time he showed up at the court, and at his insistence, two clerks who had some extra time on their hands visited his apartment, where they found his jacket pockets stuffed with ticket stubs, and videos, all around his television, of every Nazi movie that one could ever rent or see. When they played one titled *The Room,* one of the actors delivered Hans's exact same line about the room. His TV didn't even work except to show these videos. He owned action flicks, the comic-book film versions, Holocaust epics, documentaries, stories of one regular man in times of horror, and stories of one extraordinary man in times of horror. He could've opened a specialized movie store.

They filed their report and sent him

home. "You're just a regular man," they told him. "Congratulations."

2.

This Hoefler, he stayed away for a month or so, but then he brought himself back to the court again. And again. He became their regular monthly visitor. The judge enjoyed seeing him, but he was unsure what to do with him, so he telephoned his niece, who was studying psychology and had talked about needing someone to test, and she in turn set up a mock Milgram obedience test for Hans, for her Ethics and History class.

She put Hans in a room in the classic situation, in which he had to shock a victim, played by an actor, with a false electrical current, while a pretend supervisor claimed to assume responsibility for the victim's screams of pain. She employed various friends from graduate school — the Psychology and Theatre Departments — and in truth, it was one of their most fun collaborations, and led to a very vital discussion the following week about grandparents. The test helped explain why cruelty was so easy to indulge if responsibility was claimed by someone else, but, caught off guard, on a regular workday, as his regular self, Hans Hoefler refused to use the shocking equipment, and he walked out, shaking his head, blinking as if he'd been stunned himself. When he returned to the court, pale as ever, the judge hailed his clerk, who called his niece, who drove over right away and ran in with the video to show Hans the recording of his own decency. Of his own interior strength. It was a slow afternoon, and everyone in the court office stood around the TV, watching him watch, hopeful. "You passed!" crowed the clerk.

Hans, as if deaf, made no sound.

"This is good, Hans," the stout judge said kindly, the judge who, by then, had grown a strong affection for Hans Hoefler; after seeing criminal after criminal denying his crime, screwing up his or her face and saying, It is *not* me, I would never do such a thing, here was Hans, scooping up what was not his and cradling it like a child. Hans Hoefler, with his heavy sad eyes, who reminded the judge somewhat of his own father, dead the previous year of complications from a liver transplant.

From his viewing seat in the jury box, Hans gripped the wooden pew and said nothing as he watched himself with no expression on his face. They found him a week later, hanging from a rope in his dingy Munich apartment, with a short note propped on the dresser saying he had to die for what he had done to the Jews, to the Gypsies, to the Poles. He had piles of writing on his desk, next to the note, titled, in careful calligraphy: *One Nazi's Confessions.* In cramped handwriting, rigid black ink, Hans had written pages upon pages; he had invented instances, written of places and times that did not exist and heinous acts that had never happened. He was a revisionist but backwards, adding horrors instead of denying them, inserting himself wrongly into true events. He used familiar names and terms — Kristallnacht, Dachau, the "sweet smell" — but the details he used otherwise were often shockingly wrong. He wrote of a hurricane at Dachau. He said in Auschwitz the guards were all named Hans, which seemed like a joke, except that all who knew Hans knew his sense of humor was limited. Was he making fun of us? asked the judge, scratching his head. Of history? It's not funny, he said, and his secretary said no, she didn't think so, though she could not explain it either. Hans said that he had rounded up Jews and Gypsies in a church and burned them inside and he could not forgive himself for shooting the ones that flew out the window in an attempt to escape. But someone noted that this was awfully close to the plot of the Wiesenthal classic on forgiveness, *The Sunflower,* and that that Nazi in question was already named. It took ten minutes to find *The Sunflower* on Hans's bookshelf, dog-eared to a beige softness.

Hans's notes were bound and filed in the judge's paperwork, the finishing chapter of the Hoefler saga, which had been ongoing for more than four years by that point. "Case closed," said the judge, with no small pang of regret for having asked his niece to do the Milgram study. He had known that Hans would walk out of the test. He'd been sure of it. But if he'd known that, he should have also known that that kind of empirical evidence on videotape might clash too intensely with Hans's own image of himself as a murderer, which then might unsettle him enough to lead to something worse, but the judge was never a very good chess player and could not think nine steps ahead. It was tiring and difficult, this judge business.

Since Hans had no friends at that stage of his life, his funeral was attended only by the staff of the court. "If only the rest could be so responsible," said the auburn-haired secretary to the judge's clerk as they drank cups of stiff coffee afterward, standing in the coatroom, still in their coats. The world, they agreed, needed more Hans Hoeflers.

"Better to commit suicide than kill someone else," they suggested, but the words sat flat in their mouths as they worked that day. Like soda, unfizzed.

Even if it was true, there was something despicable about valuing Hans's concave heart, and by the end of the day, the judge's clerk found herself spurning Hans, and flicking him from her mind like a bug.

3.

That auburn-haired secretary did not flick him from her mind; instead, she drew him closer inside it. She became obsessed with what had been wrong with Hans. Why hang himself? Why all the guards named his name? What would cause a person to distort so profoundly? She was about thirty years old, and her life had fallen into predictability, and so these thoughts of Hans would not leave her mind, which was as open as a bowl, ready to receive them.

She dreamed of him all the time, walking through the streets with a cane like her father's, trailed by a tangle of scruffy dogs. Her father, a man so quiet and unobtrusive he often had been handed people's plates and trash — even in public, even out dining. There was a generation of German men who, in response to what history had re-

101

vealed, refused to tolerate any sign of internal aggression. Her father had never raised his voice. He would not even laugh loudly. He said, "I'm sorry," when people bumped into him on the street, as if his presence on the sidewalk deserved apology, for had he not been there in the first place, he reasoned, the person would have had no one to bump into. "I am a mouse, a mouse," he had whispered to her as he was dying. The problem was that being a mouse sometimes made people irritable, and many raised their voices in her father's presence because he spoke so softly it was aggravating. "I CAN'T HEAR YOU!" her mother said, often. "SPEAK LOUDER, MAN!" While he was dying, which took a few days, the nurse kept leaving her mystery novel on his stomach, along with her purse, and sometimes her snack, so when the secretary visited he was covered with objects, breathing thinly and carefully so as not to shake anything off.

Hans joined her father's ghost-space easily. The two men walked through her dreams together, unable to speak, shoulders folding in, followed by dogs. She couldn't stop thinking about them. Once, she had yelled at her mother about something small, like clothes, or the telephone, and her father had stumbled in, weeping and whispering, "Stop it!" His exclamation point came in the form of a loud *hush,* like a radiator expelling heat. She and her mother had looked over, startled. They both liked fighting. It felt like a good workout, somewhat aerobic. German women had a different legacy to manage.

Through leads on her computer and in the phone book, the secretary tried to find living Hoefler relatives, but no one returned her phone calls. Finally, through an advertisement she placed on the Internet, she was able to track down a former girlfriend of Hans's, from their courtship in the 1950s, when Germany was split in half like a bread roll; when the Ottoman Empire could still occasionally be found on globes in third-hand trinket shops.

The secretary walked up a dark stairway, curling around to the back of the stone building. The walls smelled of wine, and mold.

"The curious thing about Hans," said the woman, after introductions had been made and she was now curled on her sofa with bubbly water in a green glass on a coaster of cork, "is that he would not let me perform what many men enjoyed. That is," she said, petting the long-haired white cat who'd hopped onto her lap, "what men often request. I assume you know what I mean?"

The secretary thought of several things. Which was it? The older woman leaned in. "With the mouth," she whispered, tapping her chin with a long red fingernail. "Just that.

"He never allowed it. He did let me once, and then he insisted on serving me repeatedly for days. It was very pleasant for me," she said. "Were you similarly treated? You're awfully young."

The secretary frowned. "No," she said. "He was only an acquaintance."

"Is he dead?"

The secretary picked at the old chocolates in a silver dish between them, their corners whitened and chalky with time. She removed one and took a cautious bite. Crystallized maple sugar inside.

"Yes," she said. "I'm sorry. I should've said so earlier."

The cat closed its eyes, and no one took a sip of anything, and the sugar was sticky and too sweet in the secretary's mouth.

The older woman reached out a hand and put it on the secretary's elbow. It was a light touch, but there was something else in it. "Let me show you something," she said. She lifted the cat onto her shoulder and led the younger woman into her bedroom, which smelled musty, windows shut forever, and even with the lamp lit, had an undefeatable dimness. No direct sunlight, only the reflection of it off the building's bricks next door. It made the secretary instantly weary.

The older woman knelt, and from a drawer next to her bed removed a small gold locket. Inside was a lock of hair.

"It's my hair," she said. "Not Hans's. I soaked it in a deadly poison. Hair is porous. Had I needed to, I would've eaten it and died. We all had to have a plan."

"How old were you? Can a person eat hair?" asked the secretary, who stood awkwardly by the bed, and felt that she was being lied to.

"Of course," said the woman, dangling the hair over her mouth. "You young people don't understand. You think all poison is in a bottle. I was a very bright child."

"I am trying," said the secretary, "it's just —"

"Look," said the woman, waving the hair. "Look, yes?"

And because she knew she was supposed to, the secretary stepped up and pushed down the older woman's hand, though she was tempted to let the woman eat the hair, to call the bluff, to shut down the opera. By her estimation, the woman had probably been five years old during the height of the war. Listening to panicked voices in the next room. The majority of the living memories now owned by then-children.

The older woman began laughing; her shirt had lost its top button, purposefully or not, and you could see her skin under the luminous blouse, the settled wrinkles, the breasts, which struck the secretary as almost intolerably lonely.

"Hans was lousy," said the woman, slipping the hair back into the locket. "He was lousy and he was wonderful. He was lousy, he was wonderful, and he was a self-centered bastard."

She clipped the locket shut and announced that the secretary was no fun. "You should be wearing more textures," she suggested. "Your face is too plain for standard cotton." She stood and rummaged in her closet and returned with a brightly colored silk-and-sheep's-wool scarf, tasseled at the ends. "Wear it," she said. The secretary waved her hand. "Wear it," said the woman. The secretary opened her mouth to protest, and the woman said: "Put it on, or I will call the police and tell them that you broke into my apartment."

So it was that the secretary left the build-

ing, her coppery hair wrapped in the burgundy, ochre, and forest-green scarf, which
did become her small precise features, and
which did protect against the cold creeping
in from the north in a streamy wind. She
knew nothing new about Hans except that
he did not invite fellatio when he was a
young man and he had loved a woman as
flamboyant in her inventions as he. They
both had been so young. It said very little
to her. Now she had a new scarf and a
strange feeling in her hands and thoughts,
as if the poison had somehow crept from
the woman's lock of hair into her, and so,
when she was suitably far away, she found
the first person who looked cold, handed
her the scarf, and said take it, and that
person, whoever it was, took it, because it
was gorgeous, and because it was warm.

The secretary's own family had survived
the war, but barely. All her men had slotted
into different ages than were required. They
did not have to fight; they were either too
old or too young. Her grandfather, her
father, her brother, her first love. This
generational split freed them all from making any of the torturous decisions that Hans
Hoefler had made for himself regardless.
They formed their identities in the negative
space instead.

4.

The judge's secretary was typing one day, details about a couple out walking who had been robbed at gunpoint, a fairly unusual crime for these quiet streets, when she received a call. "I hear you want information on Hoefler," a man's voice said.

She held her fingers above the keyboard, as if typing would scare off the voice. "Yes," she said. "Please."

"Meet me at the cemetery," he told her. "Twenty minutes."

"Which cemetery?" she asked, but she knew as soon as she said it, and the man had hung up. It was only a five-minute walk, and Hans was buried there.

She finished up the tail end of the report, swallowed herself inside her coat, and walked the ten blocks east, past the pawn shop and the bakery that specialized in crusty rolls soaked in chicken fat and sesame seeds. When she arrived at Hans's grave, apprehensive, holding out her sharpest key just in case, she saw from a distance a man in a wheelchair with no hair on his head, wheeling past the headstones over the small green hills. She lowered the key. The air was chilly but clear, a good day to be outside. As the man drew closer, she saw he had no eyebrows, no eyelashes, and that he looked over seventy. She watched him navigate the bumps of grass. He did not look like the kind of man who would appreciate an offer of help.

Nearby stood other mourners, and even through the cold, she could smell the hints of the first dandelion tufts pushing their way to the surface. The man wheeled right up to Hans's headstone and nodded at her. His face was geometrically compelling, with its triangular cheekbones and rectangular forehead. She waited for him to speak.

The man thanked her for meeting him. He said he was Hoefler's brother. His older brother. He inquired after her interest and she explained that it was not professional. "I just think about him," she said. "I'm not sure why."

The man in the wheelchair sniffed in assent. "Good," he said. "Then I would like you to know a few things." He dusted his hands on the wheels of his chair, a gesture she could tell he did often. He kept his gaze on the headstone.

"When I was thirteen and Hans nine," he began, in a voice louder than was necessary, "I told him my mind was stronger than his. We had been fighting often, or I had been fighting and he had been silent, and I was tired of it, so I sat him down and told him to try to hurt me with his thoughts. He was not a violent young man, and I could see he was uncomfortable, but he tended to do anything I asked, and he stared at me willingly. Even then, he had eyes very big and dark and more like a dog's than a man's. You recall?" He glanced up and the secretary nodded. She recalled very well, she said.

"You were his lover?" the man asked, lips harsh.

For the second time that month, the woman shook her head. "I was really only a distant acquaintance," she said.

"To be stared at by Hans," the man continued, "made you want to feed him soup, not harm him. Hans thought for a long period of time, and finally took a breath and said he wished I would not always have the first glass of juice. I told him that was an idiotic curse. Almost embarrassing. Just who was this brother of mine, so shiftless in his negativity? I'd been the clear favorite of both our parents and I'd gotten all the extra gifts and sweets. I'd never caught Hans looking at me with any kind of hatred or envy, something I found disconcerting. He tried again, and said that perhaps one day I might lose all the hot water while I was inside the shower, covered with soap. I believe then I reached out and hit him. 'Come on, brother!' I said. 'Curse me! Curse me flat out!' "

The man shifted in his chair. His eyes flicked over to the woman, but not long enough to register an expression.

"Well," he said, "something inside the combination of my contempt and that slap did alter Hans a bit, did snap him into a new place. He had always been obedient, and he continued to stare with that wet Hans gaze, but when he finally spoke, he said, in a quieter voice, that he might wish I had no legs. I was by then already a very fine and fast runner in school. He said Mother would not like me so well without legs, which, I must add as a side note, turned out, unfortunately, to be true. 'Good one, Hans!' I told him, encouragingly. 'More!' He leaned closer and in a whisper said that he wished that all my hair would fall out, as we'd just seen a horror film in which the vampire's eldest child, the preferred child, loses all its hair and becomes a human snake and eats its father. Also, I had the better hair, the hair all the relatives commented upon. Such lustrous hair, too good for a boy, they all said, about my eyelashes too."

The man in the wheelchair blinked, reptilian.

"I was — to be frank — delighted," he said, leaning in. "Now, this was the sort of conversation I felt rivalrous brothers should have, and I suppose I felt guilty for all the preferential treatment I'd received, so it seemed better to get it all out in the open. I couldn't tell if Hans had cursed me because he really felt it or just to please me, but I didn't care. Of course, I was not to be outdone, and told him that he would turn scaly and dry up like a desert, that he would lose his hearing on the day of his piano recital, and forget how to speak at a crucial moment in his life, whenever that was. I said to him, 'One day you will open your mouth when it is imperative that you use it, and nothing will come out.' We were sitting in the room off of the kitchen; it was a small, dark hallway that was always warm from the heating vent, and smelled of nuts, though no one ate nuts in our home. We always loved sitting there. I was fidgety with pleasure. Hans nodded, digesting my curses. I asked for one more. His eyes began to glaze over, and he told me, as if in a trance, that Germany would collapse with me inside it, and I would be legless, dragging my body through the burning streets of a formerly beautiful city, and I would call and call and no one would come, and how I would find my darling wife dead in the flames.

"He and I sat silent then, until he shook himself alert.

" 'Will that do?' Hans asked, smiling a little shyly at me."

The man raised his forehead where his eyebrows would be.

"Well, he was quite a bit happier for a while after that," the man said. "It was probably the longest I'd spoken with him in a number of months. It's good for brothers to do a little cursing every now and then. Good to have some room to vent. All was well until, of course, the curses started to come true. The final ones didn't. I was married for ten years, later, yes, but she left me because she fell in love with a younger man. I had no darling wife, dead. I was not present at any bombing.

"But the rest did," he said. "We said so many curses that day, and the world was in such tumult that the odds were high that something would stick. None stuck to him; most did to me. Now, I knew an incident with a train took my legs, not Hans. I tended to put myself in dangerous situations. A fire took the hair off my head and eyebrows, a fire I could have avoided. But either way, though it was years later, Hans thought he had ordered it all, straight off a menu from the devil himself, and although I told him it was not his fault, he surely thought otherwise. That there was both greatness and a terrible danger in his mind."

A light wind blew through the cemetery. The secretary kept her weight on both feet. She felt a bit too tall, taller than she liked to feel, but she did not want to sit on the grass, as it was wet.

"Never once did I think it was the power of his mind," Hans's brother said. "He had a fine human mind, sure, but he was no soothsayer. Please. I told him that, too — 'You're just a regular kid, Hans!' — but I'm sure he thought I was trying to placate him. He read the news daily, every single word. It was a terrible time, a terrifying time. We could hardly understand any of it. And I felt terrible that I had encouraged him so. I was older; I should've known better. He hadn't wanted to say anything, and I had made him, and then things came true, and imagination met reality. We all knew some-one who had done something. News kept pouring in. Poor Hans. He listened to it all with terror. He stopped seeing his friends. It wasn't just him; many young men I knew who had frightening thoughts or dreams were extremely vigilant in those days. One neighbor went on serious drugs to sleep so he'd stop having some kind of dream; he never said what it was. We did not know what we were capable of. The lid was off.

"I even once told him to curse me again, or to bless me — his choice — but by then he was a very different kind of man."

He hummed lightly. The mourners on either side huddled back to their cars in the dimming light and drove away.

"And, you know," he said, sighing, "it's not true that nothing stuck to him. In a way, my curses came true too. In a metaphorical way. That moment of speechlessness happened to him over and over, where he could not talk when it was of tantamount importance. He rarely talked at all. He never married or truly fell in love. He never did anything with his life. Just wandered from country to country. We lost touch many years ago."

The man closed his mouth, and the two looked at the headstone together, reading and rereading the few words there: *Hans Hoefler,* and the quote they had decided upon as a group at the court: *We need more Hans Hoeflers in this world.*

The words looked wrong, like a carving of incorrect dates. The secretary pulled her coat tighter around herself. She thought of how she had never sat and had a long conversation with her father because he, too, refused to talk about himself. "Someone else should speak instead," he said. "If I don't speak, it means someone else will," which did not always turn out to be true. She spent many, many hours with him in an expectant silence. *"Tell me,"* she whispered, softly, sometimes, but he would just look at her mildly, a flat blankness in his eyes. He did not even shake his head; it was like words had returned to abstraction to him, just interesting sounds exiting the mouth of the young woman whose nose and hands reminded him of something.

At the cemetery, she stepped closer and touched the shoulder of the man in the wheelchair, and he reached up to her hand with his own. He was much older, and hairless, but the bones in his face were still handsome. Compared with Hans — worried, dark-eyed Hans — this chair-bound brother still received more appreciative looks from women. There was something broad and fine in the way his cheekbones paralleled his jaw. The secretary walked next to him, and helped him home without seeming like she was helping, and stood with him in the elevator, and accompanied him into his apartment, into rooms that were clean and spare. Without words, as if they had been married for years, the two commenced cooking dinner together, chopping carrots and onions, warming the bread. He showed her a photo album of his childhood, and she could see the hair he had described and the strong legs of the former athlete. They ate facing the window, though it was night, and watched the lights in the building across the street switch on one by one. "Delicious," he said once, and she nodded.

Before she left, after stacking the dishes and snapping off squares of dark chocolate from the cupboard, she pulled her chair in closer to him and, placing a hand on each of his shoulders, kissed his cheeks, his head, the heavy flat bones of his eyebrows where no hair grew. She kissed near his lips, but not on them. His eyelids closed, and she kissed their round, soft orbs. Each fingertip. Each palm. The corner where his jaw hinged, and the light lobe of his ear.

"I am too old —" he began, and she shushed him. She took his weathered, hairless hand, and placed it gently inside her shirt, on her breast, and she just let him hold her there, listening to her heart beat. In some quiet basic way, it was the opposite of the scarf given to her by the old woman the previous month. Here was a tasselless moment, without instruction or order or guilt or implication.

"Thank you for calling me," she said, and she loosened the bowl of his palm, and said good night. His eyes were closed then. Not asleep, just cupping the tears that had gathered under the lids. She let herself out. The night was windy but clear, and since she had already eaten dinner, earlier than expected, the time felt unusually spacious. She stepped into a music club and listened to a violinist play Bach while a piano player waited his turn, and she sipped a glass of wine so acidic it seized her throat lightly, and she thought of the man who was sleeping now, and although she still dreamed of both of them often, she never investigated into Hans again.

5.

The story would be over about Hans Hoefler except for one piece.

The week after the secretary's visit, the brother decided to return to the grave; something about her visit made him want to go back.

It was a gray-skied October morning, and the brother wheeled over the knots of grass to the headstone, where he stared at Hans's name for at least half an hour.

It is difficult to want to tell a grave that it is not immortal. It's so obvious at that point. And yet the brother wheeled as close as he could, and, leaning down from his chair, he grasped the cold sides of the headstone with his hands.

"You weren't that powerful, kid," he cried. "You died, didn't you?"

And yet, even as he said it, he realized, with new clarity, that Hans had killed himself. And that it did not seem like an act of fear or great despair. It seemed almost like some sort of trick. The vampire's child, from that horror film, had been a creature thousands of years old. Perhaps Hans had thought he would live forever, would curse and be cursed forever, would rule the world with his mind, forever. No one could ever prove to Hans now that he was as mortal and helpless as the rest. He had circumvented the question.

It altered the taste of the brother's spit, thinking this. He took his hands off the headstone and wheeled away. It was beginning to rain anyway, and a heady mossy smell overtook the grassy hills of the cemetery. He wheeled as quickly as he could, past the chapel, through the iron gates, to the steadying relief of slick wheels on hard concrete. He popped open his umbrella and fixed it to the arm of his wheelchair. The rain was loud and pointed.

Had we left him here, the bitterness would be where we saw him last and maybe where he died, for wherever we see him last is where we assume he will stay forever. But we will not leave him there. Soon after the visit, his mouth relaxed, and within a week, there were tears, and the tears changed the muscles of his face, because they were not bitter tears but tears of sadness — sadness at the parents who had died long before, tears for Hans and his desperate delusions, tears for his country's impossible recovery, tears for the fact that life happened once and choices were exactly what they were. Hans was still dead. The world went on perfectly fine without him, just as the war had started, happened, and ended without his playing a role as either hero or villain. One could not spend one's life in the imaginings of another life; if the brother spent too much time with that, the wheelchair would crowd out all other thoughts. So he poured himself a glass of cold coffee from the coffee jug which he had put, unlidded, into the refrigerator, and the caffeine relaxed him, clarified his sight, as he looked out the window into the rainy afternoon. He would not call the auburn-haired woman who had been so kind, because what they had shared had been completed. But he could keep his eyes open now for the next point of meaning. He could watch the sky all day long. He could return to the restaurant with the fine herb omelettes where he had deliberately left his umbrella because he hadn't wanted to leave. There was love to be felt, and discovered, still. There was a powerlessness that was kind.

LEMONADE

I was at the Bev with Sylv and we were eating Chinese food takeout from Panda Express and I said about how the chicken chow mein would be a good street, like Chow Main? Like a Main Street in a food part of town? Get it? And then Sylv said she had to go to the bathroom and she left for a really long time. And I got nervous because she was gone too long and I thought maybe she'd even left the mall. Because maybe she is part Chinese and I just didn't know? Her hair is black. And maybe I had totally offended her with my Chow Main Street idea; Mein and Main are not the same and here's me, trying to make the Chinese into something American, and that is offensive, right, like I was that loud American taking over all the Chinese words, like saying it was Ciao Main or something, like Italian Chinese? And Chow is our word for eat — chow — but in China it's probably something really different. So I was feeling really bad and really racist by accident and she came back and sat down and it had been I swear twenty minutes? and I said, Sylvia, I just wanted to say I'm really, really sorry about the Chow Main comment, and she looked at me through her new blue eyeliner which I noticed just then and said, What? And I said, Just I didn't mean to offend you with the using of Mein as Main, I know that's different, and she said, I don't know what you're talking about, Louanne. And she took a big sip of her Diet Coke. Behind her, by the movie theatre, two girls from school who are bitches strolled by; Sylv didn't see, she was going on about how she'd checked her messages and Jack hadn't called even though he said he would but maybe he was caught in traffic. Even though he has a phone? But I'd never say that out loud. Sylv's the first friend I've had in a long time who really is way high on the friend pyramid, and the way she dances! She bops around really energetically but she's also still. Like she's moving her torso but her feet don't move, and then sometimes she'll take one step, and it feels like a thesis state-ment. Like it is a topic sentence about her butt.

And then I couldn't help it, I made another Chinese joke! Because I said that the popcorn shrimp would be good to take to the movies. And she was quiet and I thought: Oh my God, I did it again, didn't I? Why do I do that? And I was about to say I was really sorry again when her cell rang and I could tell it was Jack because her whole face got all shimmery. It made me feel a little bad, actually, to see her face change like that. Because I think I'm pretty good company and I even have a few jokes I keep stored in my mind just in case there's nothing to say but from the look on her face it was like she was released from jail. And she giggled to Jack, and I thought maybe the popcorn shrimp joke was okay because there were no Chinese words in it? And did she have a Chinese cousin somewhere or what? But it didn't matter if she did or not because this is America so she should be offended anyway, on behalf of America. I should have offended myself. And I just thought maybe it was in bad taste, because movie popcorn is an old tradition but doesn't take a whole lot of skill but popcorn shrimp, for all I know, could be passed down from many years of Chinese cooking classes and generations only to show up here at the Bev food court for all of us to enjoy. I really liked mine. I ate it all and it was kind of sparky in my mouth and then I ate two of hers, and I would've eaten more but she gave me that look with her eyebrow up and then she threw them out in the trash, which was hard for me just because they're so delicious, but I wasn't going to pick them out of the garbage or anything. Even though the garbage looked pretty clean.

Before we left the food court, I made a point of waving to the cute little Chinese food lady over at Panda Express who was wearing a chef's hat, just in case she'd heard me, but she didn't see me waving anyway because she was serving orange chicken in a rice bowl to some old guy who probably didn't appreciate her good service at all.

When Sylv got off the phone she said Jack would meet us downstairs at the MAC store, so we took the escalators down, and I was feeling kind of gross from the popcorn shrimp but still I wanted to eat more so I had this weird balance of feeling like sleeping and also like eating for another hour, and then going up the escalator in the other direction were those two girls from school again, and Sylv saw them and hissed, Did you see? It's Barb and Nature, and it was and is; I do not like Nature, she was a bitch to me in fifth grade when we were partners together on the make-the-book-diorama project and she said, Let's make a mirror into a lake for *Swan Lake,* and I said, There's no book *Swan Lake* but we can do another book with a swan, like *The Trumpeter of the Swan?* by the man who wrote *Charlotte's Web* about the spider? SOME PIG? And she said great so I read it and I made a little swan out of Fimo clay which had even that red stripe on the beak that all swans all have but everyone forgets. And I was supposed to go to her house to finish it but when I did she opened the door like why was I there. And I held up the clay swan and made a trumpet sound and she said, Why are you here? And I said, For our book project? and she pulled twenty dollars out of her pocket like they were magic jeans that worked like an ATM machine, and she said, Can you just finish it for both of us, please, Louellen? Lou*anne,* I said, and her eyes were all tired and droopy and slitty. Did you even read the book? I asked, and she said, Take the money and run, kid. And I took it, not because I wanted it but because she told me to take it and because she called me kid which was nice in a weird way even though we were and are the same age. Nature is like that; you just sort of do what she says because her hair is that shiny light swaying-field color that makes your brain get all puffy. Like it turns your brain into yeast. I didn't look at her as she went up the up escalator and I don't remember what I spent that twenty dollars on but we got an A on the project even though Mrs. Humfield took me aside and asked me directly if it had been uneven, the work sharing, and I said no, it was all exactly even, and Mrs. Humfield sipped out of her mug that had a hippo on it which I thought was a bad idea for a teacher who is not super skinny. Last month Nature sent a valentine to Sylvia saying Let's Be Best Buds! with a drawing of a pot leaf on it, but Sylv didn't answer which I thought was so cool. Except then Sylvia and her do sometimes stop to talk in the hall which means I wait behind and look at the sky. But the sky is interesting, it changes all the time.

And then, because everything happens at the same time, Jack came bounding up as we hit the bottom of the escalator and he grabbed Sylv and kissed her right in front of me which is okay but I saw his tongue going into her mouth and that is just disgusting. And then they walked ahead arm in arm and I thought about the boyfriend that I am going to have; he's going to go to a different school. I'll meet him by accident in a crosswalk. And then I walked by a pretty black lady in pink high heels and I forgot to smile at her which means she might've thought that I didn't smile at her because I am racist because, in case she happened to notice, I smile at everyone. I turned around to smile at her retroactively but she was walking ahead, fast, swinging her bag from Restoration Hardware. Maybe she bought herself a new faucet for her sink that makes the water really smooth. I think it's good to smile at everybody so that everyone knows you love everyone. It's good for human pacifism. That's why I even smile at people who give me mean looks, like just then there was a man with long mucky red hair without any bags walking by who looked really mad at the world, really fucked up, but we were heading over to Macy's to try on makeup and I smiled at him, too. He looked surprised; probably no one ever smiles at him anymore. I might be the first person who smiled at him in like thirty years. Definitely the first girl. I like to smile at the men who look mean so they know I believe in their better selves. That makes a difference in the world. This is how you might be able to reform a possible rapist without ever going to psychology school.

In front of the Gap, Sylvia and Jack stopped at a bench and fell into it and they just made out right there. And we were right near Macy's and right around then I started to remember deep down somewhere in my head that there are no windows here at the Beverly Center. I went over and made a little ahem sound but they couldn't hear me and I sort of watched Jack's hand go over Sylvia's shoulder and he was almost on her boob. There are two pregnant girls in school but they are both still in classes and they said how they're fat as an excuse but I can tell it's not regular fat especially because one of them is spending all her class time knitting a blue bootee. I only have kissed two guys and even then it was short, not a long time. And Sylvia seemed pretty good at it and I couldn't really stop watching and then Barb and Nature walked up swinging their shopping bags and they went over and stood right over the bench and Nature said "AHEM!" just like I did only a hundred times louder and Sylvia pulled her face away from Jack's and her mouth was all smudged and soft-looking and she laughed and said "Hi!" And they hugged. Even though didn't we all just not see each other deliberately on the escalator? And Barb was quiet but she made a naughty scoldy look at Jack and I went over and no one really looked at me but I stood there too because I was Sylvia's ride. So, if people were cars, in a way, I was the one kissing Jack, if you were to think of it that way. And Nature was talking about some party and Jack pulled Sylvia into his lap so there was bench room and Nature sat down and crossed her legs and waggled her foot around and her toes were painted dark red like she was forty years old, and then it was just me and Barb standing there and Barb said she wanted to go look at the new Gap sweaters with the zipper front. Barb is independent like that. She's taking an independent-study class in school to learn Portuguese which you'd think would make her ineligible for popularity. Did you know they speak Portuguese in Brazil? I don't understand why that is. And I stood there and Nature was holding Sylvia's hand and Jack kept grabbing it back, and then Nature took it again and they were like a sculpture: *Bad Homework Partner plus My Friend plus Her Boyfriend on Mall Bench.*

"We've been here for hours," I said.

"What?"

"We've been here since three," I said.

"I had to get some presents," said Sylvia,

leaning her head back onto Jack's shoulder.

"How are you, Louanne?" Nature asked me.

"Me?" I said. "I'm fine. How are you?"

Nature laughed, and she brought Sylvia's hand to her mouth and kissed its back. She was wearing light-pink lipstick from the MAC store and it left an imprint like on an old CD cover. Sylv laughed her little tinkling laugh. Jack made a whimpering sound.

"Now you can get into the bar," said Nature to Sylvia, holding up her imprinted hand.

"What bar?" I said.

"The Nature Bar," said Nature, and everyone but me laughed. Then she looked back up at me, with her snappy brown eyes.

"Will you leave us alone for half an hour, Louanne?"

"Alone at the Bev?" I said.

Sylvia laughed.

"The Bev?" said Nature.

I blushed. "The mall?"

"Just for a half hour," Nature said. "I need to talk to Sylvia and Jack about something important. I'll tell you another time, I just have to talk to them alone right now."

I checked my watch. Four-thirty.

"Five?" I said.

"Great," said Nature, and her hair fell into

131

her face like a curtain saying, Go home, Louanne, the corn is growing, the show is done.

I went into a fancy dress store where I could stand at the window and watch because were they all going to make out? But Nature just sat there holding Sylvia's hand and Jack at one point kissed Sylvia's neck and it was all so great for Sylvia. At one point, Barb came back with a big Gap bag and pulled out a purple zipper sweater to show them, and then left. She left? And then they all laughed on the bench for a while and after about ten minutes they got up to go. I knew they were going before they even got up. I'm not stupid. Nature was walking off with her hand in Sylvia's butt pocket and Jack was by himself but he had a car.

I was Sylvia's ride but she had two more rides now except Nature doesn't drive a car because she got her license revoked because the story goes that she was driving on Franklin and she hit a raccoon and that would be okay except she got so freaked out she ran to the nearest house crying and sobbing and said she'd hit a person and they ran out to look, all scared and calling 911, but then it was a much smaller shape on the road and one with circles around its eyes and fur and paws and a snout. And then everyone thought it meant she should take a break from driving because she was clearly high on something, to think a raccoon was a person. They are really different. The sales-lady at the store asked me if I wanted to try on that jacket, the one I was next to that I'd been petting for almost twenty minutes. It was a mink maybe? But faux fur. It was sort of a golden color, like a golden retriever. I said okay. She had to undo the cord which meant it's expensive but I tried it on like it was the animal I killed while driving high and now I couldn't drive either. So how would I get home? I'd have to wear my road kill home through the sparkly streets of Los Angeles. But it didn't look good on me because my face is splotchy sometimes and it made me extra splotchy to have fur around it. Nature said she's happy not driving because it's so nice to get driven, like she's a movie star in a limo, but everyone in school talked about the raccoon story for at least a week, and for a while people held up animals in the hall for her and said, Nature, is this a person? and it'd be a stuffed Snoopy. Or: Nature, is this a person? and it'd be an address book.

I went back and sat at the bench for ten minutes. They weren't coming back. I knew that. I wanted to do my part anyway. I smiled at people walking by. An old man with overalls walked by; I don't think old people should wear overalls; it makes them look like shrivelly toddlers. But I smiled at him anyway. Most teenage girls don't give old people the time of day which is sad because all old people do all the time is think about how nice it was to be a teenager so long ago. After a minute, he came and circled back and he was wearing overalls and that little Jewish disc hat, and sat down. He smelled like cashews.

"Are you here alone?" he asked.

"I'm a quarter Jewish," I told him. "I attend Yom Kippur services."

"Good for you," he said.

"My dad's mom," I said.

I smiled at him again, but the truth is, the smile is best when you're walking, not sitting. Sitting, I wasn't sure how long I could hold it.

"I'm meeting friends," I said.

"Are you lost?" he said.

"Oh no," I said. "I am extremely found."

"That's good," he said. He had a piece of paper in his hand and he kept folding it and unfolding it.

"Are you lost?" I asked, because maybe he had Alzheimer's.

"Sometimes," he said.

"You're on the first floor of the Beverly Center mall in Los Angeles, California," I said.

"That part I do know," he said. "But thank you."

My ten minutes of waiting was up, so I said bye and walked away from the Gap and went to the MAC store. I found the pink lipstick that looked close to what Nature was wearing and I wiped it off with a tissue because people who have herpes or chapped lips try on lipstick too, there's no ethical standard. It wasn't any good on me. It made me look even splotchier because the lipstick matched my splotch tone so it highlighted the splotches. But the saleslady wanted my money so she kept quiet and when I told her I'd buy it, she said "Great!" She said it was one of the most popular colors. It was named Electric Seashell. Which I thought was a bad name because if you put together a seashell and electricity, you could get electrocuted, depending on the location. She put it in a little MAC bag, and when I stepped out of the store, there they all were. All three of them, boom. Sculpture upright.

"Hey, Louanne," said Sylvia.

"Nice lipstick," Nature said, and I sort of blushed a little, and looked in the bag, at the lipstick case and the name, like I forgot it was there.

"Electric Seashell," I said, and I didn't know why I felt like they had caught me somehow. They were the ones that left the bench.

Nature fiddled in her pocket and pulled out a lipstick and read hers. "Electric Seashell," she said. "What do you know?" Behind her, Jack stuck his hand down Sylvia's shirt.

"Hey," said Nature, spinning hers up. It was almost flat. "I'm low on mine."

"Your what?"

"My lipstick," she said. She stepped up to me and I had this feeling like she was going to hit me, right here at the Beverly Center, with no windows, by the new café area with the indoor hedges. I never took Tae Kwon Do. But she stepped closer than a hitter would, and then she kissed me. Right in front of the MAC store. My third kiss in my life so far. She pushed her lips against mine, sort of hard, smearing them around. She smelled like tea, not cashews. Then she let go of my shoulders and stepped back, and Electric Seashell was all over her mouth and it's so perfect on her, it's raspberry jam on her stalky hair and her skin is all butter and I know cannibals are disgusting but still.

136

Her face was a scone. "Thanks," she said. And Sylvia was laughing and laughing behind her, saying, "Louanne, you should see your face!" but I can't ever see my face, I'm in my face, and then Nature said, "Thanks, Louanne, now I'm all dressed and ready to go," and they all turned around and walked off together and Jack started telling a story because he was making his arms out like an airplane. Her lips were gentle, Nature, even though she pushed them really hard. Way gentler than you would think her lips would be, being that she is Nature.

The old overalls man walked by, walking slow.

It got me thinking, for a second, about what would happen if Nature did hit a person in the road. She'd run to the neighbors and say she'd hit a telephone pole, or a rat. And no one would think it was a big deal and everyone would have a cup of tea and make the call to Triple A and stroll out to look at the damage to the car, and then there'd be a person, dead in the road, bloody, no pole at all, but a person who might've lived if only Nature had known it was a person ten minutes before.

I felt a little wave of downness then, for a second, like I might just fall on the floor of the Bev and not be able to do anything for a long time, so I walked as fast as I could and got a lemonade from the hot-dog/lemonade stand and I smiled at the balding Arab man who makes the lemonade and told him it was delicious, before I'd tasted it, actually, and he said thanks, bobbing his shiny head, and I could see him thinking what a nice thoughtful teenage girl, who takes the time to compliment lemonade and doesn't assume he's a terrorist when most teenage American girls are just busy thinking only of themselves.

"Enjoy," he said, handing over the straw.

It was okay lemonade. Not delicious, but not bad. Still, meeting him and drinking it gave me enough of a lift that I could get myself to the elevator in front of Victoria's Secret which was having a big sale on pink bras that said PRETTY over the boobs, PRE on one boob, TTY on the other.

When I was out of eyeshot, I tossed the lemonade.

I took the elevator to P3, which was the right level, and then my car was in G2, which was green, and which I had remembered by thinking GIRL, I am a GIRL, and the 2 was for TWO GIRLS: Louanne and Sylvia, going to the mall.

"G2," I'd told Sylvia, pointing it out,

explaining, as we got out of the car. "You and me," I said.

She'd shaken her head and laughed. "You are so weird, Louanne," she said, but she didn't shake me off when I linked my arm with hers.

G1, going home.

At the bottom, I paid my parking dollar and said gracias to the Mexican lady who worked the booth and I told her I liked her red earrings. She sort of stared past me with eyes that said there are more cars waiting, so I moved on ahead and made a right turn, out of the mall.

The people were all busy in their cars, listening to the radio, so there was no one to smile at, so I just sent my love to the traffic lights. No one ever appreciates them, all day long, working so hard to turn red and yellow and green, right in time with us to make sure we don't crash into each other. If there was any tiny chance, even the tiniest chance, that they happened to be alive, I bet I was the first person ever to tell them they were special. You are special, I said out loud in my car, but in case they couldn't hear, I cracked my window open. "You are special," I said, to the night air.

And just like that, a green light.

And then it's me and La Cienega, all the way home.

BAD RETURN

I met Arlene in college, in the freshman dorm. We were not roommates but suite-mates in the corner section of a squat brick house at the center of a small college campus in the middle of Ohio. We both had moved from opposite coasts with the desire for a personalized liberal-arts college experience and had become friends due to proximity and availability more than compatibility. For example, we had nothing in common. She: Blue Ridge Mountain town. Me: central California suburbs. She: declared international-relations major with three eclectic minors. Me: not yet totally decided. The men she liked were brutish jocks; I had located within two weeks every single soulful gentleman on campus who wrote poetry. I found them by the length of their hair or the wear of their jeans. She liked big-budget romantic movies; I saw every documentary I could find at the library, and if I'd had any retention ability, I would've stored a great deal of knowledge about the world. She had a perpetual perm, because she felt it added volume to the thinness of her hair and gave her a look of energy; I was hard-pressed to use a brush because I preferred a ponytail, and part of trying to attract those poet-men was to look a little like I had wandered onto campus by accident after having spent ten years with the wolves behind some farmhouse, living off scraps and reveling in the pure air like a half–girl Mowgli, half–woman Thoreau.

Unfortunately for me, she seemed to get a lot more sex than I did. The brutish jocks were hell-bent on getting her into bed, perm and all, and half of the poets — who were not really poets but just had volumes of very nice leather-bound, nearly blank poetry books given to them by parents who were trying to be supportive, books partially filled with the same poem, over and over, called "Life" and/or "Life II" and/or "Why Love Is an Illusion" — these men didn't always want to touch a woman, or a man, but, rather, mostly themselves. It took me until senior year to find a poet who actually wrote poetry, and he took off my clothes very gently and spent nearly an hour on my neck and back, and when we were done and I felt all my waiting had been worth it, he explained that part of his education as a poet was to meet as many women as possible, and so this was now to be goodbye. He suggested I pretend he was going off to war on a boat. "What boat?" I said, clutching the blanket. "We live in Ohio." He left a leaflet on my bed torn from a three-ring binder. *Your breasts are fortune cookies, full of small wisdoms,* he wrote. I read it multiple times. I almost notified the English Department. I was very tempted to show Arlene, but she was busily documenting her outings and weekends in a photo album labeled *College, Senior Year,* and although she had never been anything but sympathetic about my history with men, I couldn't bear the thought that she might laugh at me and not him.

One afternoon in late March of our senior year, just about two months before graduation, I wandered into the apartment I then shared with Arlene and found her standing at the fridge looking upset. She was rummaging around in the vegetable drawer, and her mascara was smudged. Mascara, like the perm, was part of her daily wear.

"What is it?" I said. "Is it Fred?" Fred was her latest jock, a wide-eyed, hurdle-jumping track star whom I found very attractive and who stoked my envy. I always harbored a secret hope that they'd break up.

"No," she said, into the shelves. "Fred's fine."

"And?"

"I don't know," she said. "The usual."

She held up several thin plastic bags holding vegetables we'd bought and forgotten to eat: floppy green onions, a browning head of broccoli, limp kale.

"We never ate any of this," she said.

"So throw it out," I said.

She dragged a hand across her eyes. "This happens every time," she said, shutting the fridge door. "Why do we even bother to go shopping?" She pulled on a coat and went outside with a shovel, picking and digging at the ground until she was able to bury the old vegetables under a bedraggled marigold plant. I watched from the window. She was often upset in these days, usually about graduating. Every night, she cried a little about the end of this phase of her life. What the changes would be like. How much she would miss me, and her classes, and our apartment. I would watch her cry sometimes, on the sofa with her tissue, and I'd say comforting things I'd heard other people say about the opening and closing of windows and doors, but mostly I just admired how she did it; she had this way of crying like she didn't realize she was crying.

When she came back inside, she was gripping a yogurt cup someone had thrown near our side strip of garden.

"Plastic doesn't cycle." She shrugged off her coat. "Right? We recycle it, but it can't do anything on its own, and all it can ever do is be itself again. It is the worst kind of reincarnation. Lame! That is so lame! And it's *everywhere*!" she cried, going to the bathroom to splash water on her face.

Arlene didn't usually get so worked up about things like the veggies or the yogurt cup, but her moods had been heightened in the weeks since our friend Hank had hit the doctor on his drive to the recycling plant. Hank was a nice guy who lived two apartments over with a mutt named Blooper, and the two of them came by often. Hank, like Arlene, was conscientious to a fault. In fact, he was so thorough that he did not trust that the big blue trucks would actually take his recycling to the plant, so once a week he drove it over himself. He crushed his bottles and folded up his boxes, and he said he found it very comforting to see the plant itself, those manmade cycles in action. "It's called a *plant*!" he'd say, goofily, delighted. Had he not been gay, I'm sure he and Arlene would have fallen very deeply in love for a long time.

One afternoon, while on his drive to the recycling plant, Hank glanced down at the radio during a song he didn't like and hit a doctor. The doctor, a young surgeon just finishing his residency, was crossing the road on a sunny afternoon on his lunch break, and he stepped into the street right when Hank was spinning the tuning dial. Hank knocked him to the ground, and the tires rolled over his hands. The doctor who had specialized in surgery for children with cancer.

Arlene did not appreciate my line of thinking.

"You cannot make an equation!" she said, coming out of the bathroom. "The doctor's hands did not break because Hank was recycling!"

She adjusted the ribbon on her dress that she was wearing as a gesture of support for Hank, who was meeting that day with a lawyer.

"True," I said, flicking on the light that she always flicked off, even when we were studying. "And yet, if Hank did not feel the need to drive his bags to the plant, then the doctor would be fine. Correct?"

"That's fudging the data!" Arlene protested.

The doorbell rang. Fred came in. He was looking particularly strong and flushed that evening, having just finished lifting weights at the gym.

"It's just so sad," I said. "He saved children."

"It's horribly sad," Arlene said. "But it is not a lesson. Hey, baby." She turned away from me and leaned in to give Fred a kiss.

"Or how about the Litmans?" I said.

The Litmans were the liberal parents of a mutual friend of ours who had adopted a homeless kid with no family and raised him with love and care and good limits and kind gifts and progressive schools, and the kid had grown up to be a staunch ultra-right neo-con who believed in torture and wiretapping civilians and aggressive, preemptive warfare. The parents did not know what to do.

Arlene began to rub Fred's shoulders. "Did you go to the gym?" she said. "You look hot."

"Nice dress," he said.

"Anyway," she said to me. "You can't predict the outcome. You can't raise a kid and then tell him what to think."

"No," I said. "I'm just saying."

"You're saying we should all stay at home and do nothing," she said.

"Claire's not a shut-in," Fred said, smiling at me.

"See?" I said, smiling back, although Arlene's statement did sound a little true.

"What happened with Hank and the lawyer?" he asked.

"I don't know," Arlene said. "He's still not back." She held on to the sides of his T-shirt. Her eyes filled with real tears. Fred kissed the top of her head tenderly, and for the umpteenth time, I wondered how Arlene, of the questionably toxic perms and mascara drips and yogurt cup righteousness, always got the better guys.

"He has to live with that his whole life," she said.

Fred ran a hand through her hair. They left, to go to dinner.

"I hate you people," I muttered as I shoved my eggshells into our small kitchen compost pile, which smelled like rotten food, which is just exactly what it was.

The building quieted around me. Saturday night. I had nothing to do. The latest guy I'd liked, a documentary filmmaker, had to work late in the editing room. I loved documentaries, but he said I couldn't see his for two more months, and, like a sports star, he said it was better that he work solo and think solo until he was done. Due to dating choices such as this, I seemed to have more time than most of my peers, so I had pursued an addiction to crossword puzzles. When not studying, I opened up the newspaper and did the daily one each afternoon. I was not particularly good, and often could not answer the questions. I grabbed a pencil and curled up on the sofa and opened the newspaper to the puzzle I'd started the night before. As I worked away, rereading the same clues, two thoughts commonly accompanied my work. One was my strong desire to finish as quickly as possible so I could do something else, who knew what. But finishing quickly was impossible, so I also found myself thinking that if someday I were taken by a dictatorship and shoved into a holding tank with only this crossword, and my only chance for survival was to finish this crossword, then and only then might I be able to figure out the answer to 12D: Lincoln's controversial Cabinet member. Maybe it would take years, I considered, skipping that question, but as I continued to work the puzzle, I could feel that holding tank floating in the background, an

Orwellian-style setup with a large crossword projected onto the wall as the world warred outside, and for some reason the future of humanity might even depend on whether or not I could plumb the depths of old history tests in my memory, and rustle up the answers.

Maybe then, I thought to myself, primly, I could finish.

I did the crossword for a while, made a tiny bit of progress by asserting that Plato was Greek, and then wandered out onto campus. I didn't feel like seeing the new movie or going to the new specialty-beer bar that had just opened up across the street.

Instead, I found myself pulled to the main quad of campus, an area of green that, with spring, was only just starting to lighten and brighten from beneath the layers of cold, dark wetness. Some kind of vigil was going on. Rows and rows of students were sitting with candles, wearing gloves and hats. It was colder than I'd expected. I was shivering in my coat and scarf, and Julian, the documentary maker, was tucked warm in a dark room with technology, and Arlene and Fred were going to "dinner," which often meant they were just waiting for me to leave so they could return to the apartment and have loud sex. Twice I'd come home as they were finishing, and, honestly, I cannot think of a lonelier sound on a Saturday night than one's roommate having a giant orgasm and then making an embarrassed *sssh* sound, realizing that maybe through the fog of her pleasure she'd heard the front door open and close.

So there I was, at this vigil. I knelt down. A man on a podium was talking.

"What's it for?" I whispered to two women wrapped up together in a bright-blue sleeping bag.

"The war," they said.

"Which one?"

"All of them," they said.

"How many are there?" I said.

One shrugged. "At least three."

I tried to count the wars in my head. I could count two.

"What's the third?" I hissed.

"Sssh!" said the sleeping-bag pair, in unison.

"So," said the man at the podium, a man with a beard and a knit cap, "as murderers, we too should be punished. Look around! Look harder! Look at what you're not seeing!"

"Why are we murderers?" I whispered to the two.

"Duh," said one.

"It's a wake-up call," said the other. "Most of us forget we're even at war at all."

I nodded. In fact, I could hardly hold the thought about forgetting in my head. It seemed destined to be forgotten.

"Brring!" said the man at the podium. "I am your inner alarm clock. Brrring!"

The group rose to its feet and began marching, with candles, down the main walkway of campus. The duo, bundled in their sleeping bag, moved in a lump ahead of me. I began walking too. I knew no one in the war/wars and hardly thought about them, and when I did, I wore the guilt and outrage like an accessory I could remove the same way as a nice pair of earrings. I would let the outrage adorn and better me and then slide the wires from my earlobes and tuck them away in my jewelry box. I felt ashamed of this even as I did it over and over, and one could reasonably argue that the fact that I felt ashamed about it and still did it made it worse. At least the Litman kid had beliefs.

We walked in clumps, heads leaning forward. Was there a group plan? Should I call my one journalism friend? But more than anything, I was pulled by the movement of something happening, something where I could join a flow and participate in some way without notice.

We walked for fifteen minutes, and at times the man from the podium, now with a megaphone, would call out "Murderers!" and the crowd would respond "Yes!" and then the feet would pick up. I hid my face in my scarf.

On campus a few weeks earlier, there had been a real protest, a sincere protest, one I had attended with Arlene, who did seem able to remember that we were at war and had adopted a soldier online to whom she sent electrolyte-enhanced water and peanut butter cups and moisturizer for the desert. She wrote him long letters in response to his letters and once even spoke to his wife on the phone to make it clear she was not flirting. "I have a great boyfriend," I heard her say, as I was walking into the room to retrieve my latest attempt at the crossword. "Fred." She was tugging at a curl, and her brow was furrowed with concentration and concern. "I truly mean no disrespect," she said. At that sincere protest, with Arlene shouting next to me, our shouts visible in puffs of cold, I'd felt a momentary crush of panic, like for one second I got it, grasped the stakes, understood that people my age were living a completely different and precarious life on my watch, but then it was over and the crowd dispersed and we went to have potato skins at the food co-op. "But what's a person to do?" I'd asked Arlene, scooping up fake bacon bits with a bit of crisped peel. "Give up everything?"

She dabbed her mouth with a napkin. It was just the two of us. Fred was away at a track meet in Akron.

"No-o," she said, slowly. "Give up something?"

At this second rally, I continued to follow the sleeping-bag twins as they rustled along the sidewalk. This protest had a completely different feel than the last one, more like we were sleepwalking into a dream where death was only a Jungian symbol made into a colorful illustration on a tarot card. It was, by now, probably ten-thirty, and the regents were asleep in their white houses. We walked off campus, down a residential street to an empty dirt lot buttressed by two tract homes. Soon the lot would grow a house that exactly matched the ones on either side.

"Go!" said the man with the megaphone.

It was like watching a dance in slow motion. As if they'd all planned it in advance, which clearly most of them had, the marchers began shedding their clothes. The night was thirty or forty degrees, probably less, but off came the sleeping bags, the sweat-shirts, the hats, the scarves, the shoes. I wasn't sure what any of it had to do with dead soldiers, but it certainly was interest-ing. "Off!" yelled the man, and soon there were over a hundred naked coeds, their clothes in heaps. "Show your true selves!" he yelled, and they put their bodies on the lot, which I now realized was probably the largest plot of dirt around, since the campus was covered in concrete, brick, and grass, and all the students rolled in the dirt — "This is what we need!" he said — and they were rolling, and kissing, and kicking aside clothes, and warming up skin on skin, and shivering, trying to reclaim a decade long past. I was now standing in the veranda of the next-door neighbor's house, which, as far as I could tell, had a still-up neighbor in it, due to the flickering light of the flat-screen TV I could see through sheer white curtains. Did the neighbor know that one hundred nubile twenty-year-olds were roll-ing in the dirt next door? I thought not. It seemed he was watching *Law & Order.*

The man with the megaphone backed off. He watched the bodies rolling and reach-ing. He watched piles of bodies start kiss-ing. He saw me over in the veranda and glanced at me for a moment, I suppose to

155

see if I was the type to tell. And it seemed he decided no, because then he began to pick his way through the bodies and clothing and with nimble, practiced fingers lifted over fifty wallets from the stack, tossing them into his backpack. Sighs and grunts erupted around him as he threaded through the piles and then tiptoed away. He'd read me right; I didn't say a word. It seemed, in its way, a fair exchange.

When I woke up, the lot was clear. No naked bodies, no police, just one leftover sock in the dirt, lit by the white disc of moon. I'd fallen asleep sprawled out on the porch with my scarf wrapped tightly over my head. It was cold out, but tiredness had overtaken me, swallowed me, as it sometimes did, and so I hadn't gotten to see the marchers finishing, or getting dressed, or yelling about their wallets.

I blew on my hands. Stretched. The whole elaborate thing — from protest to empty lot — had done nothing but make me irritable. There were real deaths happening, after all. Hard to imagine from our dorm apartments and fifty-minute course lectures. And on a pettier and slightly more distracting level, I also didn't like having stood, as always, so everlastingly, to the side. I was certainly not doing my share to help out the world in any way, and neither was I doing my share by having fun as a naked college coed. I was basically sleeping through all of it. Was I really a nothing-doer, an apathetic blob? Was Arlene right? She planned most of our weekend activities. She adopted the soldier and called the wife. She had sex with Fred. When people danced at weddings, I would stand on the side grimacing, but not because I did not want to dance. I just couldn't seem to. Cousins and happy types would cheerfully grab my hands and draw me into the center, but even with that encouragement, with smiles like fields of daisies surrounding, I could only make it through half a song. The magnet inside the wall was too strong. I liked Julian, tucked in his documentary office; he was the perfect boyfriend for me, similar to that magnet — someone I could not touch but who, with a pull from beneath a surface, still kept me from the activities at hand.

This all left me so cold and cranky that I decided right then and there to make something happen, because it is always possible to make something happen, and there was no reason that I had to go home right then with my hands jammed in my pockets and say hi to Arlene and Fred all cuddled up warm watching late-night comedy TV with their hair so mussed and gleaming and not have participated in anything myself. It was this reason, and perhaps others I did not understand, that led me to turn to the front door of the house attached to the porch upon which I was standing, square my shoulders, and knock.

By then it was well after midnight. The same flicker of TV light still broke against the windowpanes, but I didn't even know if the watcher was awake until he quickly bounded up to the door.

"Yes?" said the voice, through the door. A male voice: reedy, elderly.

"I'm sorry to bother you," I said. "Did you see what happened?"

"Something happened?" He pulled back the flimsy curtains that covered the window in the center of the door. He was an older man, probably close to sixty-five. Whitish hair. Bushy eyebrows that could've commanded authority but on his face brought to mind squirrels and hairbrushes. He could've been my grandfather, except my grandfathers were robust men, who strode through the world and stepped on people, including both of my parents.

"A hundred people were robbed right next to you," I said, through the glass. "While having sex."

"Robbed?" He looked startled. "Here? Sex?"

"While you were watching *Law & Order,*" I said.

He let go of the curtain and opened the door. He was shorter than I was. Although I was female and he male, I felt very clearly that I was the threat in this situation.

"Did someone call the police?" he said. "Are you a student?"

"No police," I said, waving behind me, at the dark emptiness. "I'm a student."

He stared. He was observing me as keenly as I was observing him. I could see the observations floating through his face, him observing, me observing him observing.

Finally he asked, "Would you like to come in?"

He didn't seem scary, and the house looked warm. He led me through the living room. It was inviting, with the flat-screen TV nestled above the fireplace and lavish plants in metal holders marking the corners, everything tidy and clutterless, but not in an oppressive way. In the kitchen, he put on a kettle without asking, which I appreciated. It seemed we both understood that if I didn't like tea I just wouldn't drink it.

The kitchen had pale-green tile and light

wooden cabinets. I made a note of the placement of the knife block, just in case.

He prepared a Japanese barley tea as my hands and cheeks thawed.

"I lived in Kyoto for many years," he said when the water was ready, pouring the mugs full. "And I drank this every day. Not the same here. There, it's fresh, roasted. Here, it was packed long ago. Whispers."

He tilted his head to the sitting area, by the window overlooking the empty lot.

"They're building a new house there, supposedly," he said, handing over my mug. "It's been three years."

We sat down and looked out the window together, at the leftover sock.

"That's where it happened," I said, taking a sip.

"They all had sex?" he said.

"A hundred of them."

"And then?"

"The guy stole their wallets."

"What guy?"

"The guy who told them to have sex on Mother Earth as a war protest."

"Ah," he said, nodding.

"You didn't hear anything?"

"Not a thing."

"I fell asleep," I admitted.

We sat and sipped, the warm tea spread-

160

ing through my chest. Barley tea. It felt good to be doing something. Not that I was quite sure what I was doing. I tried to think up an interesting question to ask him, maybe about his childhood, or his first love, or if he'd fought in any war, when he turned to face me, his squirrel eyebrows up. By then most adults would've launched into their usual list of annoying questions — my major, my plans for the future, my hopes and dreams — but he just raised a hand and poked at the air between us, as if to poke those questions aside.

"Was it a good episode?" I asked.

"Of?"

Law & Order," I said.

He shrugged. "I'd seen it before."

He poked again at the air between us. Raised his hand, dusted the air aside, put his hand down. Waited. Raised his hand again, pushed at the air, put his hand down again.

"What are you doing?" I asked, trying to laugh.

When he did it again, I raised my hand back. While he dusted the air on one side, I dusted the opposing side. I pushed some air at him. He smiled. Pushed it back.

"Could you do me a favor?" he asked.

"Depends," I said.

He indicated upstairs with his chin. "I need a lightbulb changed in the guest room," he said. "You're taller than I am."

It was true; I was. I looked at the flight of stairs past the kitchen, the dim light above. It was a small two-story house, probably two bedrooms upstairs, one his, one guest. No sign of a cat, dog, or any other resident. A lightbulb. It was, by all accounts, dumb to go upstairs in the house of someone I did not know, especially a male stranger's house at one in the morning. With everyone nearby fast asleep. That said, I still felt that if anyone were at risk, it was actually him; I'd trusted what I'd read about following my own fear instinct, and instead of feeling fear, what I felt was a slight thrill or even a flicker of aggression, like I might harm him, like *he* should be cautious about inviting *me* up.

"It's a dumb idea," I said, sniffing. "Stranger's house."

"I'll sit right here," he said. "I won't move, I promise."

"Oldest trick in the book," I said. "Light-bulb changing."

"It is true, though," he said.

I sipped my tea. "Nah."

Still, I felt a strange and powerful pull to his second floor.

"I'll come by in the daytime with a friend," I said, "and we'll change every lightbulb you need."

"Sure, of course," he said, shrugging. "Thank you."

He refilled his cup with hot water. From our spot in the kitchen, I could make out the side frames of paintings lining the stairway walls, chosen carefully over time to represent whatever he wanted to observe while ascending. He stirred his tea.

"Okay, fine," I said, standing. "Twist my arm."

He raised his eyebrows, surprised.

"I might steal something, you know," I said.

"Go ahead," he said, warmly. "Take whatever you like. It's the first room on your left. Thank you, thank you so much."

I left my mug and climbed the stairs, past paintings of green hills dotted with trees and sheep, painted by a person named Hovick. The old man sat at the table downstairs, sipping his tea. I could hear him, sipping loudly, nearly slurping, and he had been a polite and quiet sipper earlier, so I figured he was doing it to let me know he was staying put.

"Where's the bulb?" I asked, at the top of the stairs.

"On the dresser," he called.

The room was cheerful enough — a small bedroom with a twin bed, a vase holding a graceful twig that required no water, and a lush, light-green carpet that matched the kitchen tiles. A desk lamp glowed through a sheer, paisley-patterned shade. On the dresser was the new fluorescent bulb with its squiggly spiral up, and I turned off the overhead light, stood on a wooden chair, and unscrewed the fixture. The bulb was warm. With a bit of balancing, I reached up with the new bulb and screwed it in, and on with the fixture again, and a twist and a turn, and his loud sipping below reminding me I had nothing to fear. I pushed the chair back to the desk and surveyed the room once again, my gaze settling on the bedside table, where a book about Ohio flora lay next to a fluted lamp.

"Done," I called.

"Thank you," he said, from the kitchen.

But I did not feel done. I picked up the book on Ohio flora. Inside, between pictures of dogwood trees, I found pressed petals, wrinkled and overlapping and folded, page after page. He had saved a whole bouquet. I punched the bed's pillow in the center, to make it look as if a person had slept on it at some point. It was a headless pillow, a pil-

164

low that had not made contact with a head, a sight that made me feel inexplicably angry. I moved the twig to the other side of the vase. I looked under the bed and saw two slippers lined up neatly, the kind with a band over the toes made of floral terrycloth. I shook and emptied the book of Ohio flora petals all over the bed, until it was covered in dry purple flowers, like a honeymoon bed for one.

Downstairs, the man was staring out the window.

I settled into my seat.

"Thank you," he said again. "I've heard so much talk about these fluorescent bulbs."

Some kind of mood had descended upon him while I was in the room. His voice drizzled into nowhere as he spoke.

"Whose room is that?" I asked, reaching for my tea.

"My daughter's," he said.

"Is she okay?" I asked.

He turned to me. His eyelids flickered lower. "She lives with her mother."

"Where?"

"In Egypt."

"Does she visit you?"

"No."

"Why not?"

"She is allergic to green," he said.

He was looking out the window at his little side garden again, so I looked too, at the budding spring trees, half-lit by someone's porch lamp, and at the hints of grass in the garden, peeking through winter. Soon enough, the whole town would be covered in green.

"All shades?"

"Every one," he said.

"So why don't you move to her?"

"I need it to live," he said.

"Need what?"

"Green," he said.

He turned back to the table and resumed what he had been doing before: pushing at the air with that faint, focused look on his face.

"Egypt has green," I said, squinting.

"Not much," he said. "In the southern part. Mostly browns and golds and blues."

"A person isn't allergic to a color," I said.

He kept his eyes on the air between us. "Most people are not."

I sipped my tea. I could not wait to tell all this to Arlene.

"It's not like cats," I said.

He paused, his hand on the air. "I had this idea," he said. "The other day. While drinking tea."

"Or peanuts," I said.

"While looking out this same window," he said. "I thought that if a young woman ever happened to knock on my door, I would have a job for her. That the young woman could go into Nina's room. And if she did, it would make the mark of young women and somehow it would bring her — my daughter — closer."

He sorted some air to the right, some to the left.

"I would somehow summon your daughter?"

He nodded, briskly. "The way we put flowers in a room to bring joy," he said. "The way we —" With a measured effort, he slowed his gestures and stopped messing with the air and folded his hands on the table.

I tipped back in my chair. I felt unusually comfortable in his house.

"By green, do you mean an environmental reference?" I asked.

He frowned. "No," he said. "I mean actual green."

"But, then, so what if I did summon her? She'd still be allergic, right?"

"Correct."

"And you have green tile and green carpet and green hills on the wall."

"Yes."

"And you refuse to change your décor," I said.

"I need it," he said. "With less green, I get vertigo."

"Oh, come *on,*" I said, balancing on the back chair legs. "Are you kidding? Did the lightbulb even need changing?"

"Of course," he said, "those lightbulbs last twelve times longer."

He pressed at his eyes with a napkin. I lifted my hands off the table for a second. Balanced. Swung the chair back down. "Oh," I said, "speaking of flowers. I think I may've spilled some of yours on the bed."

He finished his tea. Dabbed his mouth dry.

"There are no flowers in that room," he said.

"The dried ones in the Ohio flora book?" I said, sipping my tea.

He peered at me.

"Purple?" I said. "Purple petals?"

He rose.

"Was that bad?" I said.

We headed up together, past Hovick's pastures. As soon as he walked into the small bedroom, he knelt at the edge of the bed, his knees on the slippers, his hands clutching at the flower petals, clutching and letting go, like they were the most special thing in the world to him.

I watched for a minute. I could not tell what he was feeling. "I'm very sorry," I said. "I don't know why I did that."

He rested his cheek against the petals for a moment. "It's okay," he said, heavily.

"They're your daughter's?"

He kept his eyes closed. Shook his head. "No."

To give him some privacy, I stared at the floor. At the petals he had dropped. At the specks of gold in the green flat carpet weave. I did feel, against my will, creeping into my cheeks, a surge of what could only be called pleasure, which came from the fact that something interesting was starting to happen, something I myself had instigated, a feeling I found repellent in its selfishness but still unyielding.

"Are they from your wedding?" I asked, softly.

"No." He held a handful of petals close to his face.

A funeral, I wondered. One of his beloved parents. What a rude thing for me to do, to take something precious and throw it all over the room like that.

"No funeral," he said, as if he had read my mind. He closed his eyes. "They're from

169

nothing," he said. "They came in the book."

I nodded. "What do you mean?"

"The Ohio flora book," he said. He rested his face on the bedspread again.

"It came with flowers?"

"I found the book and inside were these flowers."

"You mean when you bought the book?"

"They were in the book when I bought it." He smoothed the petals near his hair. "I bought it used," he said, by way of explanation.

I took a step forward on the lush green carpet, careful not to crush the petals he'd dropped. "I don't understand," I said, slowly. "They're not your flowers?"

"No," he said.

"Then why are you upset?"

He opened his eyes and looked at me straight on. "Because they meant something," he said.

"To someone else."

"To someone."

He kept gathering up the petals, smoothing them over the comforter, gathering and smoothing, and as I watched him I felt the very beginning, the very tiny initial curdles of irritation start to cluster and foment inside me. Something in the house was beginning to close in on me, and my softer feelings of sympathy at his old-man isolation were starting to harden and shrink into a kernel of annoyance that emitted a vaporous cloud of what could only be called entitlement. Like I owned this house. Like I lived in it, or could, or should. Like I was there to do whatever I wanted, me making the mark for all young women, and he would not, or could not, stop any of it.

"Maybe they did come from a wedding," he said, bringing a cracked petal to his nose and sniffing it.

I walked over to the old oak dresser and pulled open the top drawer. Empty. Second drawer. Empty. Went to the nightstand drawer, by the bed. Empty.

"What is this place?" I said.

In the hallway, I opened two more doors, master bedroom, master bath, bed made, drawers closed. I turned on the lights. So neat, as if no one lived there, or wore anything, or sweated.

"What are you doing?" he called.

"Who *lives* here?" I called back.

I opened the linen closet, with its piles of fluffy towels in rows. Opened the dresser drawers in his bedroom, full of stacks of white undershirts. His nightstand drawer contained only a Bible and a comb. The Bible's spine was unbroken, a firm brick of a book, and I was surprised to see it because he had not seemed like a religious man, but more than anything devout, it reminded me of the Bibles in drawers in American hotel rooms, and I imagined this man on a business trip opening a drawer and seeing one and interpreting it as something other people did in their bedrooms, something he then came home to imitate. I felt a wave of revulsion pass through me, thick and heavy, and something else, too, something I couldn't pinpoint.

"Where's *Nina*?" I called out.

"Egypt," he mumbled, from the other room.

"I mean here," I said. "Where are the photos? Drawings? Where is anything of her at all?"

I looked behind the headboard. Nothing. Under the bed. Nothing. Opened the drawer of the other nightstand. Hearing a rattle from the back, I pulled out the drawer and flipped it over, and onto the taut bedspread fell a silver nail clipper and a ring.

"She doesn't like having her picture taken," he called from the other room. "She is unusually unphotogenic."

The nail clipper was of the same style I had in my own nightstand drawer back at the apartment. I picked it up and clipped a nail, out of habit.

"She has never enjoyed the drawing of pictures," he said.

I put down the clipper and picked up the ring.

"Too much green," he said.

I was about to say something about the drawing of pictures, how most kids would be forced to draw a picture in school at some point, even if they didn't like to, and she could do it without using green, and how most parents would save the occasional picture, even if it sucked, and put it on the wall, or on the refrigerator, when my fingers reacted to the ring I was holding. It's hard to explain. I had picked up something new, but it did not feel new.

"Hey," I said. "I know this ring."

I tried to say it in a friendly voice, but a prickle of fear traveled down the backs of my arms.

"She does send an occasional e-mail," he said.

"Sir?"

"But I do not know how to save them on the computer."

I bounced the ring around in my hand. I bounced it, to make it casual. It wasn't the most unusual ring, just the kind teenagers buy at street fairs for twelve dollars, with a silver band and a yellow-orange stone. But I'd had a ring very similar to it, extremely similar. I'd had it until just that past summer, when I'd thrown it into the Kern River as a gesture of growth.

I turned the ring over. It was the exact same size as mine. The stone had the same dullness.

"What is this?" My voice came out a little too high. I walked over to the other bedroom. "Sir?"

He glanced up from his curled position by the bed. "Perhaps you can show me," he said, "how to alter my mail settings."

I held the ring up to the light. "Where did you get this?"

He sat taller, squinting. "Is that the ring?" He beamed at me. "Oh, good! I was wondering where that was! It's not a photo, but there! There's a piece of her, right there."

"Where did this come from?"

"That's Nina's," he said. "That is Nina's ring."

"But where did she get it?"

"She gave it to me on her last visit," he said, face glowing. "She wanted me to have something of hers."

"When was her last visit?"

"Four years ago," he said.

I turned the ring over. It had a scratch on

the underside, where mine had had a scratch, too. A very, very similar, if not exact, scratch.

"This is my ring," I said.

"Oh no," he said, straightening up. "That is my daughter, Nina's. She gave it to me. She got it at a street fair."

"I threw it in the river," I said.

He frowned. "She said it was collateral, for our next meeting. She loves that ring. Reminds her of the sun."

I stared at him. He had a petal stuck to his cheek, and he looked like a boy who'd been out playing in the meadows.

"Or maybe it was five years ago," he said.

The ring slipped around in my hand, just as mine had. I'd watched it sink past the bright water, into the current.

"Have you ever been to the Kern River?" I said.

"The Corn River?" he said.

"In California. Kern."

"I've never been to California," he said. "What is that look on your face?"

I held the ring tightly. "I had a ring just like this," I said. "And I threw it in the Kern River. Last summer."

"I'm sure it was a different ring."

I opened my hand. The yellow stone deepened to orange in the upper right hemisphere; I used to call it 80 percent yellow, 20 percent orange. The same slightly tweaked setting: a band of silver, not quite symmetrical.

"I threw it in the Kern River as my way into adulthood."

He wiped the petal off his cheek, and it drifted to the carpet. "Well," he said. "I don't know what to tell you. Nina gave me that ring off her finger five years ago and told me to keep it for her until her next visit."

"But she couldn't have had it five years ago," I said.

"Why not?"

"Because I was wearing it."

"But that's just what she did," he said.

I closed my fist around the ring. "Come on! Is any of this Nina stuff even true?"

"Of course it's true!" he said, and his face washed out a little, panicked. "That's her ring."

"But this is *my* ring, too!" I waved it in the air. "Down to the scratch on the inside! Down to the shape of the stone!"

He shrank against the side of the bed. Meekly, he said something about how she'd taken it off her finger, and how she'd bought it at a street fair in Cairo, and how she didn't like to use a calendar to make plans, and his words were trembling but insistent, and I had no idea if Nina was real, or never born, or if there could be two rings exactly the same, and he finished what he was saying and slumped down against the bedspread and closed his eyes.

"She told me to keep it for her for a while," he said, in a low, hollow voice.

From outside came the distant sound of an owl. I slipped the ring onto my finger. It fit, just as it had fit before. Slightly loose, but held in place by the knuckle.

"I bought this ring at a sidewalk sale in Fresno," I said. "In high school. Age fifteen. And I wore it for five years. And then last summer I was on a trip with my family, and I threw it in the Kern River because it was finally time to grow up. I kissed the stone, said goodbye to being a kid, and threw it in. Then I cried a little and went back to join everybody."

I twisted it on my finger, as I had for years.

"Here it is again," I said.

"Do you want to keep it for now?" he asked, in a tired voice.

"No."

I slid down the door frame to sit on the carpet. I closed my eyes, too. "I'm not Nina."

"No," he said.

"I'm Claire," I said.

"Howard."

We let the names fill the room.

"Hi," I said.

"Hi."

I sat there for a while and maybe even fell asleep again for a few minutes. When I woke up, I went to his bathroom and splashed water on my face. Went to his bedroom and returned the ring to the drawer with the nail clipper. Went back to the doorway of the smaller bedroom. His head was resting on the bed of petals, and his eyes were open. He looked a little older now, heavier, quiet.

"Here." I picked up the book of Ohio flora. "Here, Howard. Come on. Let's put them back."

We spent the next half hour placing six petals per page, alongside photos of Ohio marigolds and chestnuts and elms. Many of the petals had crunched into triangles on the floor; those we swept up and put into one of the empty drawers.

After we were done, he walked me downstairs, out onto the porch, and down the steps into the star-clear coldness of night. It must have been two or three in the morning.

"Thank you for the lightbulb change," he said.

"Thanks for the tea."

He nodded. We looked out past the dirt lot to a road beyond where the houses ended. It was a road that no one drove on unless they were very specifically going to either the recycling plant where Hank had been headed or to the Russian grocery complex. Another owl hoot came rolling at us from far away.

"One more thing," he said, putting a hand on my shoulder. His voice was still low, but for some reason, now that we were out of the house, it sounded less wavery and broken than it had upstairs; its reediness reminded me of wind whistling, like its own sound now instead of a diminishment.

"Yes?"

"Drop the documentary filmmaker," he said. "Go to Arlene. Stay friends with Arlene."

I shrank under his hand. "What?"

"He's in there rolling his film, cutting and rolling, and never thinks of you," the old man said. "Not once. Not ever. She is thinking of everyone. She is a good friend. A good friend is rare. Go to her. Ed loves Arlene because she is a good person. He may have a friend, someone you'll like. Go to

Ed, ask him. Ask her. Eat dinner with them. Bury vegetables. Why not?"

He stood straighter. In the far distance, headlights rounded a corner, coming our way.

"What?" I said again, sharp.

"You don't have to start with a hundred people having sex," he said.

I watched the headlights come closer, the approach of big metal-music inside. I could have stepped into the street, flagged down the car, and asked for a ride home. The headlights illuminated the man, his elderly hunch. Then it was gone.

"Have you been stalking me?"

"No," he said, smiling a little. "You found my door, remember?"

"Did you look in my purse?"

"You don't have a purse," he said, which was true.

"Did you hunt down my ring?"

"You threw it in the river," he said. "How would I do that?"

I couldn't think up an answer. "Is this what all the air pushing was for?"

He sniffed.

"Or the tea?" I asked.

"Is just good plain barley tea." He slapped his arms from the cold, and we stared into the night together.

"By the way," I said, "it's Fred."

"Fred?"

"Arlene's guy. Is Fred, not Ed," I said, smiling at the ground.

"Fred?" he said, nodding, frowning. Then he patted my shoulder goodbye and turned to let himself back in.

When I arrived back home, Arlene was up, making late-night waffles. She did this sometimes when she couldn't sleep. Her face was scrubbed clean, and she looked smaller, and about ten times more vulnerable, without that blush on her cheeks and careful mascara.

"Hey," she whispered when I came in.

She was whisking batter in a bowl and soon would be pouring it into the new waffle iron her father had sent from his kitchen supply store in Asheville. As on most evenings, she was wearing her oldest pink bathrobe, with embroidered suns on each lapel. Her mother had embroidered those suns there, as a gift to Arlene before college. Arlene, unlike most people our age, wore it with pride. She had moved past and through its symbolism, and now to her it was just a nice bathrobe.

I leaned on the cabinets, next to her. I could hear the steady, hunky breathing of

Fred in the next room.

"How was your night?"

"Okay," I said.

She looked up, whisk in hand, brow furrowed.

"I went to a war protest."

"There was another one?" she said, disappointed.

"A bad one," I said. "A fake. I saw a hundred people have sex and then get their wallets lifted."

"No kidding?"

"And then I had tea with an old man who had dredged a river."

She raised her eyebrows, curious. I told her a brief version, leaving out the part about his daughter. I also left out that I'd gone into his house, alone, and pretended instead that I met him at a late-night teahouse.

"He dredged the river to find your ring?"

"No," I said. "I made that part up."

"I bet it was a different ring," she said.

"Looked exactly the same," I said. "Same scratch. Same silver tweak."

"Weird." She wrinkled her nose. Only then did I see that her eyes were red, and that she kept dabbing them with a wet tissue, which in clump and formation looked a whole lot like the same tissue she'd been using earlier in the day.

"You okay?"

"Yeah," she said.

"You can use a new tissue."

"It's okay," she said. "It's only water."

I didn't ask why she'd been crying. I figured she probably had a good reason.

"Arlene," I said.

"Yeah?"

I didn't know what to ask her. How to be a person? On the first day of school, she had sought me out: saw me, made a beeline, and held out her hand for hello. "You have such great hands," she had told me. My hands? She'd held one up and pointed out the shape of my fingers, the squareness, the good knuckles. "You were watching my hands?" I asked, and she said that during the orientation activity, when we had to wave at airplanes for some reason we could not recall, she had noticed my hands waving because they seemed like the hands of an interesting person. In the fall, she would be doing the Peace Corps or Teach For America, depending on which program took her first. Arlene, who made sure every used item went into the right bin because she wanted all things, everything, to find its way back into the world, new.

She was standing right next to me with

her tissue. I put my head on her shoulder. Closed my eyes. "Will we stay friends?"

"Who? You and me?"

I nodded. The room smelled like waffle batter.

"What do you mean?" she said.

Those embroidered suns lit my eyelids, shining up from her bathrobe. "We have nothing in common," I said.

"Oh, shush." She started to laugh. "Human. You human. You silly human," she said, leaning her head against mine.

ORIGIN LESSONS

We met the new teacher for origin class. He was tall, with a mustache. He was our last resort. The family-genealogy class had failed. The trip to the zoo to look at monkeys had failed. The investigation of sperm and egg in a dish had failed. All were interesting, but they were not enough. Where did the sperm come from? Where did the monkey come from? Where did Romania come from?

He sat in a chair at the front of the rug.

We began all at once, everywhere, he said.

We sat quietly, waiting.

Has he started? someone whispered.

Yes, he said. I have started. We began all at once, everywhere.

We thought about that.

But before that?

He shrugged. Goes beyond what we know, he said. All we can know is the universe.

I thought we started in a dot, someone said.

He shook his head. He brought out his lunch in a brown bag from his briefcase.

No dot, he said. A dot is at a point, and if at a point, things are also not at that point.

We watched as he chewed a baby carrot.

A very well-packed dot, someone else offered. From which all things hurled free. Not unlike a suitcase.

Nope, he said. Everywhere, all at once.

Then what? someone asked.

After that? he said. Well, at first, it was fast. Everything accelerating fast. Everything wanting to get out.

Get out of what?

Poor wording, he said. Just rapid acceleration. Then it slowed down. Now expansion is accelerating steadily.

What expansion?

Oh, the universe is expanding, he said, wiping his mouth. We found that out in 1929. From Hubble.

We nodded. This made sense. It had been in a suitcase and then —

No suitcase! he said, stomping his foot. All at once, everywhere!

Someone started to cry. Someone else pushed Martha into the rug.

How about this, he said. He put away his

lunch bag and opened his briefcase again and brought out sock puppets to show us personified matter and radiation. So, he said, what happened was that, after around four hundred thousand years, everything slowed and cooled, and matter grew lumpy due to gravity, and radiation stayed smooth. Before that, the two lived evenly together.

He wound the two socks together and then moved them away from each other, and the lumpy sock got all lumpified, ready to form galaxies, and he stuffed a battery-operated lightbulb inside the smooth sock so that the light beneath the fabric radiated.

Nice, we said.

The origin of galaxies, he said, with a flourish.

Are those your socks?

No, he said. I bought the socks at a store.

Won't the lightbulb burn the sock?

No, he said, coughing. It is a specially insulated sock.

Are we accelerating right now?

Yes, he said.

Edgar grabbed on to his seat. I feel it! he shouted. He fell off his chair.

The teacher removed the socks from his hands. We can't feel it, he said. But everything is moving away from everything else, and it does mean that, in a few billion years, even our beautiful neighbors may be drifting out of reach.

He looked sad, saying that. We felt a sadness. In a billion years, our beautiful neighbors pulling away. But, surely, we will not be here in a billion years. Surely we will be something new, something that might not conceive of distance in the same way. We told him this, and he nodded, but it was wistful.

He had set up a telescope on a corner of the roof, and we went up to take a look.

This is time travel, he said, narrowing an eye to set the lens. Because the light is old. We're seeing back in time.

No, we said, wrinkling our noses. We are seeing right now, today.

No, he said, the light has to travel to us and it takes millions of years. What you're seeing is time.

Excuse me, we said. We were embarrassed to correct him. He seemed so smart. What we're seeing is space.

It's space, yes, he said. It's also time. You're seeing what has already happened.

That's absurd, we said, though we did not move.

We make bigger telescopes, radio telescopes, he said, to see back all the way. We can go back thirteen billion years now!

Almost to the Big Bang.

No, we said.

Yes!

You can see all that way back?

Yes!

And? we said, sitting up. The suitcase?

We pictured it at the end of a telescope. The longest, biggest telescope ever made. A tiny suitcase, of a pleasing brown leather.

Well, he said, leaning on the side wall. We can see very close to the beginning, but at around 400,000 years, the universe goes opaque.

We almost tossed him off the roof then. We were right there at the edge.

It's true, he said. We can see all the way to about year 400,000! Can you believe that? But before that, it's veiled.

We stopped to consider this. The universe began in a veil.

Like a bride? we said.

He smiled for the first time that day.

Sure, he said, relenting. Like a bride.

And she takes off her veil at 400,000?

She does, he said. We see her quite well after that.

So who'd she marry? we ask, settling ourselves at his feet. When a bride removes her veil, it's the moment of marriage.

189

I don't know, he said, scratching his head.
Everything? Us?

THE DOCTOR AND THE RABBI

The doctor went to see the rabbi. "Tell me, rabbi, please," he said, "about God."

The rabbi pulled out some books. She talked about Jacob, wrestling the angel. She talked about Heschel and the kernel of wonder as a seedling that could grow into awe. She tugged at her braid and told a Hassidic story about how it is said that at the end of your life you will need to apologize to God for the ways you have not lived.

"Not for the usual sins," she said. "For the sin of living small."

The doctor sat in his suit in his chair and fidgeted. Although he had initiated the conversation, he found the word "God" offensive, the same way he disliked it when people spoke about remodeling their kitchens.

"I'm sorry," he said, standing. "I cannot seem to understand what you are saying. Are you speaking English?"

"English?" said the rabbi, closing a book. Dust motes floated off the pages into the room and caught the light as they glided upward. She wrinkled her forehead as if she was double-checking in there. "Yes," she said.

A few months later, the rabbi became sick. She had a disease of the blood, a disease that needed weekly transfusions that she scheduled on Wednesdays so she would be at her best for Shabbat.

The doctor who had come to see her was a doctor of blood. A transfusionist. He had chosen this profession because blood was at the center of all of it. It was either blood, or the heart, or the brain. Or the lungs. He picked blood because it was everywhere. He was never even slightly interested in skin, or feet, joints, or even genitals. It was the most central core stuff of life and death that made him tolerate all those god-awful courses in anatomy and biochemistry.

She thought of him as she sat with her husband, staring at their enfolded hands, wondering what to do.

"That man," she said, looking up. "That man who came by a few months ago."

When the rabbi was in her paper gown she looked smaller, of the earth, and the doctor did not mind the role reversal.

"I'm so sorry you have to go through this," he said.

The rabbi lay down on the cold table. She offered her arm. The blood drained from her; the blood of another person filled her. The doctor stood beside her and reset the instruments in a line.

The rabbi came for many transfusions, and she recovered at a brisk pace, filled with the blood of Hindus and Lutherans. The treatments went so well she didn't have to visit as often anymore, and the doctor missed seeing her at the clinic. After a month had gone by, he went to her office again, where he found her talking to another rabbi, massaging the bottom of a stockinged foot. He stood outside the door as she sifted through her shelves, finding a book, opening it to a page, the two rabbis huddled shoulder to shoulder, commenting, gesturing. The age-old activity of Jews.

The doctor stayed near the door. He was not one to interrupt.

It was when the rabbi was locking up that she glanced over and saw him. Her color was back. Her eyes were clear. She was an attractive woman, with a kind, bearish husband, one raven-haired child, pink dots of warmth in the centers of her cheeks. She hugged him, and pressed his hand, and thanked him, and he said he would like to talk to her again.

"About God?" she asked.

"I'm not sure," he said. "I don't think so."

They went to a coffee shop, because she could now go no longer than two hours without food.

She asked him why blood. He explained. The river of it. They picked at a croissant on wax paper between them. The radio expelled old pop songs. He felt something stir inside him when beside her, but it was not lust, and it was not religion. What was it? "I feel a stirring when I sit with you," he said, rolling his coffee mug in his hands. "But it is not lustful."

"I'm married," she said, as an afterthought. She had bright-blue clay earrings on, formed into the shapes of stars.

"It's like the coffee tastes more like coffee," he said.

She sipped hers.

"There's good coffee here," she said.

"It's not that."

There was a pause. He found it awkward. She did not seem to mind. She dipped a croissant end into her coffee, and the buttery layers soaked up the warmth.

"I gave you the blood of other religions," he blurted.

She laughed out loud, lifting out the croissant. "No problem," she said. "I like what you gave me. It's great. How'd you know?"

"There's a box on the donation form," he said. "An optional box."

"Ah," she nodded.

"I went with those who had checked the optional box."

"How interesting that it's a box on a form," she said, chewing. "I've never heard of that before."

He scratched his nose. "It's new."

"Hospital rules?"

"No."

"Who made the form?"

"Me," he said.

"You can do that?"

"Sure." He shrugged. "No one thinks to question an extra form. Plus, it's optional."

"So — who'd I get?" she asked, now dipping the croissant torso.

His hands were shaking, slightly. He put them flat on the table, to calm them. He wasn't sure why he was so nervous around her.

"Christians," he said. "Of all sorts. Including a Jehovah's Witness. Several Muslims. A few Jews."

"Maybe it's a new route to world peace," she said. "Transfuse people."

"And atheists?" he said, tentatively.

"What about them?"

"I gave you atheist blood, too," he said. He cringed, visibly.

She laughed again. All that warmth in her laugh, like it could embrace someone across a room.

"I don't hate the atheists," she said.

"I'm an atheist," he said, a little too loud, and he reached out for her hand.

For a second, she held his. His hand was much wider than hers, and her hands, not usually considered dainty, looked small and slender next to his.

"I'm not here to push anything on you," she said. "Lots of Jews I know are atheist Jews."

"Your eyes shine," he said. "How do they do that?"

"Blood," she said.

They slipped into the affair, even though it was not an affair. It was never anything to do with losing clothes. It was not the deep sharing of feelings. It was almost entirely one-sided. It was simple, like he'd slipped slightly into her blood, and she slipped strongly into his thinking. She had one or two dreams in which he played a part, as a kind of helpful direction-giver when lost on a highway, dreams she was only mildly aware of when she woke up and went to shower.

For the most part, she focused on the congregants who needed comfort, and her husband and young son with the amazing brown eyes. The doctor, however, cultivated thoughts of her like a fresh little garden. Sometimes he pulled out her chart just to reread her basic stats, because the numbers brought him something akin to joy. To joy, really — the numbers lifted his heart and step, buoyed his day. It was just knowing this person was alive, he thought. That he had helped her, maybe even saved her, and now she was out there talking about all this business he did not believe in.

God, he said, in his car, driving from hospital to home. What a word. Much had been made already of its similarity to "dog," but as he wound through the streets, he particularly enjoyed conjuring up the image in his head of some kind of old and glowing man on a leash.

Not that he believed in such things, but he wondered if giving her atheist blood might in fact turn her into an atheist, and he felt guilty at the thought but also pleased

— like she could come over to his house and they could browse his bookshelves, shoulder to shoulder, and read Sartre together, or a dash of Camus, and then stand on chairs in old-fashioned hats and drop apples from great heights to the floor.

He returned to the rabbi's office. His mother was not well. She had cancer. She was in the hospital. Her illness had little to do with blood, or at least not his kind of blood, and so he'd stood around her hospital room, awkward, without a task. He watched the TV, attached to the ceiling with metal straps and hooks, the show pointing down upon them. He loved his mother, even though she seemed to be so private a person he had never understood much about her. She only ever told him on a daily basis about her day.

"I went to the grocery store," she would say. "I got my hair done."

"What else?" he asked once.

"I ate potato chips," she said. "I talked to your Aunt Sophie."

"About what?" he said.

She hummed, thinking. "About everything, I suppose," she said. "And how are you?"

"I'm fine," he said. "I bought a radio. But

what do you mean, everything?"

She paused on the phone. He could hear her unpacking groceries. "Sophie tells me about everything she is thinking and feeling," his mother said. "It's very interesting."

"And you?"

"I so enjoy hearing what Sophie has to say," she said.

"I have been unable to work very much this week," he told the rabbi. "I took two days off."

"Makes sense," she said. She was wearing a navy-blue suit, maybe because she had attended a funeral, or a business meeting. The daily workings of a rabbi's schedule were highly mysterious to him.

She was also surrounded by cardboard boxes of donations for a charity drive, and had just started sorting items into piles. A kid clothing pile, an adult clothing pile, a book pile, a toy pile.

"Want to help?" she asked.

"Sure." He took the free seat. She had a pile of books in her lap, and was separating them into kid and adult levels.

"And my son is not doing well, either," he said, settling in. "He lives with my ex-wife. He failed algebra."

He opened a donation box. Sweaters. The rabbi was divvying up her book piles, but he could tell she was listening. She divvied quietly.

"I tried to tutor him," he said, "but I didn't know how. I forgot algebra."

The rabbi shrugged. "Who remembers?"

"My ex-wife doesn't like to talk about it," he said. "My mother is doing a little better. They say she can go home tomorrow."

He listed all the people on his fingers. Mother, son, ex. Looked at his hands. Ham-handed, he'd been called, as a boy. Big fingers. He had turned out to be very deft with needles, which had surprised everybody.

"And how are you holding up?" the rabbi asked.

"Fine," he said.

He folded up the sweaters. Two had fairly large moth holes eating up the sleeves. "This okay?" he asked, showing her.

"Agh, no," she said. She pointed under her desk. "Ungivables."

He tossed over the sweaters, began folding others.

"What a stressful time," said the rabbi.

"You say that to all the visitors," he said, smiling a little.

She smiled back. "I still mean it."

He folded the arms in carefully, then made the sweaters into tidy squares, smoothing down the fronts, so that each one looked new, like it had just been taken from a box at a department store and placed upon a table.

"Let me ask you a question," said the rabbi, balancing the last book in the adult pile. "You're here to see me. Why?"

"Because I like seeing you."

"I like seeing you, too. But you could go to a friend. To a colleague."

"You think doctors know how to talk about this stuff?"

She pulled a pile of animal toys into her lap, including an unusually large red plastic chicken.

"Bock-bock," she said, moving the chicken up and down.

"I like seeing you," the doctor said again.

"Well," said the rabbi, steadying the chicken in her lap. "I ask because I have a rabbi kind of thing to say."

"Let's hear it," he said.

"It's not a secular comment, is what I'm saying," said the rabbi. "It will probably piss off the atheist."

"I get it, that's okay," said the doctor, pressing hands down on his pants. He placed his neat pile of sweaters in the adult pile. "I came here. Let's hear it."

She touched the plastic comb on the

chicken's head gently.

"You could pray," she said. "Either on your own, or with us."

"Oh, that?" said the doctor, shaking his head. "The 'p' word? No."

"Not to an old-man-in-the-sky kind of God," she said. "Not to solve all your problems. Just to ask for some help."

"Oh," said the doctor. "Nah. I don't do that sort of thing."

"Why not?" she said. There was no edge to her voice. Just interest.

The doctor put a small bottle of bubbles in the kid pile.

"Bubbles!" he said.

He looked back at her.

"Just because I think it's useless," he said. "And a little creepy."

She laughed. "Okay," she said. The red chicken bobbed in her lap. "Fair enough." She glanced at the adult clothes pile.

"What beautiful folding," she said.

He had opened another box and found a mushed pile of T-shirts, washed but un-folded, as if they had gone straight from the dryer into the donation box.

"And," he said, after a minute, shaking out a T-shirt, "just to play along. You know. I wouldn't want to use up the line space."

"What line space?" she said. She placed

the chicken in the kid pile. "You mean like margins?"

He swept his hand in the air. "No, a line," he said. "A line-line. Like in the post office. Let's say there's a line. Of people praying. And I added my prayer to it. Well, I don't want to take up someone else's space in line with my half-assed, half-believing, baloney prayer."

She laughed, again. Now she had a pile of very-loved stuffed animals in her lap. She was looking so well. He could not help but feel a little proud of how she was looking. He had made sure she had gotten very good blood.

"You atheists," she said. "Scratch the surface and so many of you are so old school."

He coughed. "What do you mean?"

"As if there's a line!" she said. She released the herd of stuffed animals into the kid toy pile.

"But one prayer could edge out another prayer," he said.

"I don't see how," she said.

"It's just logic!" he said. He felt the sweat beading up, on his forehead. All those sweaters, all that wool. It was May. They were doing a clothing-and-toy drive for some holiday. Tu B'Shvat? Or was that January? Wasn't that about trees? Who needed sweaters now?

"If I'm . . . praying," he said, growing a little impatient, "and there are people across the world who pray five times a day, well, I think their prayers should be heard first, before my prayer, because they have, well, 'earned' their prayer spot in line, just as I would earn my place in line if I attended a museum opening and arrived at noon with a sack lunch for a three p.m. opening. There!" he said, sitting back, folding his arms.

The rabbi leaned in. She seemed to have forgotten about the piles for the moment. Her eyes were beams of light. "But there's no line," she said.

"How do you know?"

"Well, I don't *know*," she said. "But you're using an example that doesn't fit. An example that is of this daily world. You have to think differently."

"All we know is of this world," he said.

"True," she said. "True."

The doctor sniffed. "Or don't you think the prayer lines get scrambled, with too many people praying?"

"I don't think it's like the phone system," she said.

"Why not?" He held himself tight. "Six

billion people on the planet, right? Some of them pray every day. Several times a day! All day!"

"But —" she said.

"I have no interest in cutting in the queue," he said.

"I don't think it's a merit system," she said. "Or a queue."

"But it would have to be, right?" he said. "There has to be some linear order. A way for whoever is supposedly listening to decide what to listen to first?"

She pushed her hair off her face. "I'm not sure God even has ears like that," she said.

He laughed. "Well, then, it's even more pointless than I thought!"

She paused. She was looking in the middle distance, gathering. He could see she did not want to flood him. So much flooding, alone, pouring out of her eyes.

"Go ahead," he said.

"Okay," she said, slowly. A leftover giraffe fell on the floor.

"Here," he said, picking it up.

She furrowed her forehead, thinking. Took the giraffe, absently stroked its back.

"The best way I can think to describe it," she said, "is the way, when you're driving on the freeway at night, how everyone can see the moon in their window. Every car, on the road. Every car feels the moon is following that car. Even in the other direction, right? Everyone in that entire hemisphere can see the moon and think it is there for them, is following where they go.

"You've had that experience?"

"Many times," he said. "I see the moon right out my window."

She kept petting the giraffe, as if it were a cat. Petting the little giraffe ears.

"That," she said, "is a little closer to how I imagine it works. Whether or not you pray has absolutely nothing to do with the person to your left. It's like saying you shouldn't get the moon in your window, or else the other cars wouldn't get the moon in their windows. But everyone gets the moon. It's not an option, to not have the moon in your window. You just see it. It's there."

She bit her lip. The window in the office grew golden with late afternoon.

"Half the world can't see the moon," said the doctor.

"It's not the greatest example," said the rabbi.

"Plus, the moon is far," the doctor said, brushing dryer lint off a T-shirt. "That's why everyone has access."

"True," said the rabbi.

"So is God far?"

"I don't think those distance terms apply in the same way," she said.

"Then I don't understand the example."

"It's not —" she said, clasping her hands together around the giraffe. "It's not so literal."

"I am literal," he said. "I think literally. The moon is also unresponsive."

She shook her head. "I'm sorry," she said. "It's hard to find the right example. I'm not saying pray to the moon," she said. "Truly. I'm just trying to think up a way to talk about why there's no queue, you know?"

"You don't think God has ears?"

She sat back in her chair. "Not like our ears."

He laughed, short. "I'm a doctor," he said, putting all the folded T-shirts into a neat stack.

She resettled herself. Her face was warm, flushed.

"And are these prayers to be answered?" he said.

She seemed to be resting now, the urgency quieting, and he could see her shifting modes, back to her regular rabbi self, her teacher self, returning to the statements she said maybe once a week, twice a week, to different audiences. "In Judaism we pray for a variety of reasons," she said, gently tucking the giraffe next to a few worn teddy bears. She closed her eyes. "Out of gratitude. Out of despair, asking for comfort. Out of confusion. Out of anger, in defiance. To be with. To share oneself. Not for results, tangible material results, especially on Shabbat — isn't that interesting? We're not to ask for anything tangible on Shabbat, which is, I think, one of the nicest times to pray all together."

He flashed on an image of a hamburger, at a drive-through near his home, in a tinfoil pocket.

"Right now it might be helpful," she said. "That's all I'm saying."

He wiped his hands clear on his pants. "I still think it's hokum."

"Okay," she said. She opened her eyes. Her forehead relaxed. "That's okay. I'll stop. I just wanted to talk it through with you. I'm glad you stayed."

He wiped his forehead with his sleeve. It was hot in her office.

"I apologize for being so stubborn."

"You weren't stubborn," she said, leaning over and unpeeling the tape on a new box. "You were actually pretty open. In a way, in my book, we just did it."

"Did what?"

"Prayed, in a way," she said. "Wrestled

with it."

"Why do you say that?" He sat up taller. For some reason, the thought made him angry.

"Because you're leaning in," she said, unfolding the box flaps. "Because I am tired, in a way that I recognize. Because you seem to be fighting up from under some water. Into what, I don't know. Into something. Because we were talking about it deeply," she said. "I could feel it."

"We were having an argument!" he said. He stood up, but her office was too small to pace, so he turned away, and stepped away, and found himself going through the door and going down the hall to use the bathroom. Down the long, dark, narrow hallway, with its closed office doors, and framed yarn art telling stories of the Old Testament. Once he was inside the bathroom, the motion sensor light clicked on; it was the end of the day, and no one had been in for over an hour. The space held the loneliness particular to an unused bathroom, the glare of fluorescent lights, the echo of sink and crumpling paper, the tired isolation of one person in an office building, alone, at night, working too late. He used up ten paper towels on his face and neck, until he was sufficiently dry. He washed his hands carefully in the sink. He took the back exit.

The rabbi sat in her office for forty-five minutes, unpacking the last donation boxes, to see if he would return, but he did not return, and so she shouldered her bag and walked the seven blocks home.

The doctor found his car in the parking lot, one of the last three there, and joined the flow on the street. He drove with his air-conditioner fan on full blast, into traffic as the sun set, into dusk, with the full moon rising in his rearview mirror, almost taunting him with her big presence in his car alone and every car around and none of it being how he liked to think or was interested in thinking. And yet. Why did he love the rabbi? He loved her. He got home and looked through the mail, and he had driven past the drive-through, so instead he sent out for a meatball sandwich, which he ate in pieces, because it was too unwieldy to eat all at once, and even the bread he cut into bite-sized parts. He could feel it, just feel it, the glimmer of something that he did not understand. He would never call it God. He would not call it prayer. But just beyond his sandwich, and the four TV shows he watched back to back, and his teeth brushing, and his face washing, and his nighttime reading of a magazine, and his light switching off, just the faint realization that there were many ways to live a life and that some people were living a life that was very different than his, and the way they lived was beyond him and also didn't interest him and yet he could sense it. Comfort and fear rose together inside him. Like standing in the middle of a meadow, where no one had his back.

PART THREE

I can't remember the words of things. The words for words. I have lost my words. What's this from? Is it the Internet? Texting? E-mail? I see it in kids, too; it's not an aging thing. An aging issue. I do know that at the supermarket yesterday, I asked the guy where the weighing thing was, the thing that weighs other things, flailing around with my hands, indicating, and he crumpled up his forehead and said, "You mean the scale?"

"Yes" — I said, beaming, pumping his hand — "the scale!" As if he was the winner of an SAT prize giveaway.

At the doctor's office, I told my doc that it was sore.

"What's sore?"

I pointed to my neck. "This."

"Your throat," he said.

"Of course," I said.

We went over my symptoms. He gave me a subscription.

With hand gestures, you can fill in a lot of gaps, and the words *thing* and *stuff* and *-ness* also help: *patientness* instead of *patience, fastness* instead of *speed, honestness* instead of *honesty*. With these choices, many words can be indicated, and pointing or gesticulating usually works. At the shoe store, I watched a lady walk up to the mini socks and point right at them, and the salesguy knew just what she wanted. Plus, who knows what those flimsies are called anyway.

"Cavemen point," said Susan, my neighbor, one Saturday morning. "You can always point at what you want, but you'd be returning to Neanderthal standards."

"Well, maybe we're going back to caveman times," I said, pouring a circle of wet pancake into the pan. "Tech forward, language back."

"Reverting," she said.

"What?"

"*Reverting* to caveman times."

"That's not my word choice," I said, picking up the flipper thing. "I said 'going back' on purpose. I don't like that word, *reverting*."

"If it was on purpose, then fine," she said, standing a fork on its end.

216

I flipped the pancake. "Oh, fuck off," I said.

Once the edges were all gold, I put one on her plate. A perfect goldy circle. She smiled at me. But not a thank-you smile, no: a self-satisfied one. She always looks so smug. Smug, smug, smug. I like that word very much, and I won't forget it easily.

Susan calls social Web sites silly distractions. She refuses to even look at an electronic book, because she says she must have pages, must. Fine; I read pages, too. I too enjoy the book smell everybody goes on and on about. Time for the perfumists to wake up, right? A perfume called Book? With its cologne follow-up, Newspaper? The question is, does she have to be so goddamn righteous about it? Does she have to raise her eyebrows like that, when I mention an app? She looked over my shoulder once while I was texting, which was already annoying, and when I wrote *lol* she made a very clear point to me about how I was silent and not laughing out loud, not at all. I said it was just an expression, and that I was laughing out loud inside my own mind. She rolled her eyes then, way back into her head. She's not even my girlfriend. We did sleep together once, right when I moved in, but then it sort of drizzled away. We both got busy and I woke up to the neighbor problem. The neighbor-lover problem. And, sure, fine, I do check my phone about every two minutes, but so do a lot of people, and it's better than smoking, that's what I say. It's the new, lung-safe cigarette.

"Those breathing things," a student of mine said last week, gesturing at her chest. She was trying to explain to me why she had to miss the history test. I nodded. I got it.

"Pneumonia," she said.

"You okay?"

"I think so," she said. "The doctor gave me drugs."

"Drugs?"

She thought for a second. She made that little wheeze sound. "Antirobotics?"

I couldn't help smiling. "So you will not become a robot," I said.

"Hope not," she laughed.

In the daytime, I work at a school where I teach junior-high-school history. I have been working there for eight years, since I had a crisis of identity in law school and realized I hated reading red and beige books. Teaching's way better. I teach American history, and, true, we do spend a lot of time on the Revolutionary War, more than on any other war, but junior-high-school kids like the idea of people throwing tea in the water.

You'd think in school it might be better with the words, but it's worse. When we have a good class discussion, my students will sometimes raise their hands with enthusiasticness, jumping up and down in their seats, but by the time I get around to calling on them, most of them say, "I forgot what I was going to say." A good 50 percent of the time. I have taught now for a long time and this did not happen even five years ago. It is new.

"Where did it go?" I ask.

"Where did what go?"

"Your point?"

They shrug. "Don't know," they say. They hold up their cell phones. "Sorry. We are holding a lot of small things in our heads."

"What things?" I say.

"Things," they say. "In our . . ."

They point to their heads.

"We are holding a lot of them."

I'd be irritated, except as soon as they leave I have a thing I am planning to do and I walk into the center of the room to do it and whatever it was flies away. Half my days I find myself standing in the centers of rooms.

■ ■ ■ ■

In some study, they say phones and computers are replacing our cerebral cortexes, externalizing our thoughts so that we do not need to think them — the same way certain couples will have one quiet, meeky person who trails off all the sentences and one overeager type who leaps in to finish. We're the trailer-offer, Google's our jumpy mate. Susan is worried about this, but is it so bad? Sure, Shakespeare knew ten thousand words, or a million words, just a lot of words, and he was real good at what he did, but also no women were allowed in his shows and if you got sick with pneumonia you'd just die, probably in two days, and only half the children made it to age ten. So it's a trade-off, is what I say.

Susan shook her head. "It's no trade," she said. She was over again, with wine. "Meaning," she said, "you can improve your vocabulary and still get your amoxicillin and vote. It's not like there's a checklist and for each era we only get ten helpful options, and everything else goes to shit."

"I like that word, *option*," I said.

"Are you kidding me?"

"Optional," I said. *"Opt. Opting.* Nice."

220

She poured herself a second glass of wine.

"I'm so sick of dating," she said, leaning back in her chair and lifting up her legs to sit cross-legged.

"Online?"

"Yeah," she said, sighing. "Even me. Even me, online. Fine. I hate picking a name for myself, you know? Yesterday I saw a man and his Internet name was Fido. What am I supposed to do with that?"

"What'd you name yourself?"

"Nothing."

"You have to name yourself something," I said. "Or they don't let you on the site."

She finished her wine. Eyed the bottle. I refilled both of us, so it looked like it wasn't just her.

"Wordkeeper," she said.

"Your dating name is Wordkeeper?"

"Shut up," she said.

"Sex-y," I said.

"Well, maybe to someone it will be." She took off her glasses, and touched the middle top of her nose, a geste she does that I do like.

"It has a little bit of a dom tone," I said, sipping. "Like you're hoarding all the words and you'll give them out when you feel like it. Some guys will like that."

She had her eyes closed. She was thinking

something private.

"Some guys," she said.

I went to open a bag of peanuts and poured them into a bowl. Susan and I have talked about dating since that one thing, but I have always said no. I'm not completely sure why. We're like the couple on the sitcom that has good sparks but never get together for the sake of ratings.

"You know I can't," I said, putting the bowl on the table. "I'm your neighbor."

"So?" she said. She opened her eyes. "We get along. I see you almost every day."

"Too risky."

"That is such bullshit!" she said. She glared at the table. She began to shell peanuts. "Are you just not . . . attracted?"

Susan is a good-looking woman, I'll give her that. She wears blouses with one button unbuttoned right where you'd want that to happen. Her glasses make her look like you want to take off her glasses. She gets plenty of dates, or she could, if she wanted.

"You're smug," I said. I laughed at myself, surprised.

"What do you mean?"

" 'Wordkeeper'?"

"Is smug?"

I winced. "Yeah," I said. "Kind of."

"I'm old-fashioned," she said. She swept

her shells into a little pile.

I smiled, but not an agreement smile.

She shook her head. "I don't mean to be," she said. "I just like the feeling of finding the right word in my mind and employing it. I get pleasure from that feeling. I prefer language to gesture. I figured other people might, too."

"Sure," I said.

"I don't think I'm better than you."

"It's okay. You probably are."

We sat there for a while. She liked to run her long nail down the length of each peanut and then open it up like a present.

"I suppose sex is all gesture," she said.

"Not even really gesture."

"I guess not. Not indicative at all."

"No."

She ate the peanuts. She was flushed from the wine. She wanted to take off her clothes, I could feel it, the same way she was un-dressing peanuts, and I felt it as cruel then, how I didn't want to do anything with her. Maybe cruel to both of us. But the truth is, I just felt like I had e-mail to check. I could masturbate faster. It was easier, in terms of fallout. Who wants to be in an argument with a neighbor?

She held the bottom of her wineglass down hard with her fingers, like otherwise she might just fling it across the room.

I checked my phone. Sent a couple of quick texts. After a few minutes, she left.

The phone is about the same size as a cigarette pack. It's no surprise to me that the traditional cigarette lighter in many cars has turned into the space we use to recharge our phones. They are kin. The phone, like the cigarette, lets the texter/ former smoker drop out of any social interaction for a second to get a break and make a little love to the beautiful object. We need something, people. We can't live propless.

It wouldn't bother me except it bothers me. In the shower I gave myself a test. That stuff I put in my hair for suds? Is called shampoo. The silver tray hanging over the shower top? Is a caddy. The string I use to get crap out of my teeth? Is known as dental floss. She's in my head all day, Susan, so why have sex with her too? All day I hear her chiding me.

She doesn't come over for a few days, which is unusual. On Saturday I walk up to her place. I had a dream about her and it was nice, and in the interest of living in the moment, I made a tray of chocolate-dipped strawberries. I made them Friday night. Good chocolate. Good with wine. Organic strawberries, because they are very high on the pesticide list otherwise. She opens the door.

"Yeah?" she says.

She looks tired. Her hair is less planned than usual. I step in. I give her the tray.

"You brought me these?" she says, suspicious.

"I did."

"What for?"

I was in the middle of her living room. I had had a plan, I knew that. But the rest of it had vanished.

THE COLOR MASTER

Our store was expensive, I mean Ex-Pen-Sive, as anything would be if all its requests were for clothing in the colors of natural elements. The duke wanted shoes the color of rock, so he could walk in the rock and not see his feet. He was vain that way; he did not like to see his feet. He wanted to appear, from a distance, as a floating pair of ankles. But rock, of course, is many colors. The distinction's subtle, but it is not just one plain gray, that I can promise, and in order to truly blend, it would not do to give the duke a regular pair of lovely pure-gray-dyed shoes. So we had to trek over as a group to his dukedom, a three-day trip, and take bagfuls of rocks back with us, and then use them, at the studio, as guides. I spent five hours one afternoon just staring at a rock, trying to see into its color scheme. Gray, my head kept saying. I see gray.

At the shop, in general, we build clothing

and shoes — shirts and coats, soles and heels — we treat the leather, shape and weave the cloth, and even when an item isn't ordered as a special request, one pair of shoes or one robe might cost as much as a pony or a month's food from the market stalls. Most villagers do not have this kind of money, so the bulk of our customers are royalty, or the occasional wealthy traveler riding through town who has heard rumors of our skills.

For the duke's shoes, all of us tailors and shoemakers, who numbered about twelve, were working round the clock. One man had the idea to grind bits of rock into particles and then add those particles to the dye-washing bin. This helped a little. We attended visualization seminars where we tried to imagine what it was like to be a rock, and then, quietly, after an hour of deep thought and breathing, returned to our desks and tried to insert that imagery into our decision about how long to leave the shoes in the dye bath. We felt the power of the mountain in the rock, and let that play a subtle subtextual role. And then, once the dye had reached ultimate intensity, and once the shoes were a beautiful pure gray, a rocky gray, but still gray, we summoned the Color Master.

She lives about a half mile away, in a cottage behind the scrub-oak grove. We summon her by sending off a goat down the lane, because she does not like to be disturbed by people, and the goat trots down the road and butts on the door. The Color Master set up our studio and shop in the first place, years ago; she has always done the final work. But she has been looking unwell these days. For our last project — the duchess's handbag that was supposed to look like a just-blooming rose — she wore herself out thinking about pink, and was in bed for weeks after, recovering. Dark circles ringed her eyes. She is growing older. Also, her younger brother suffers from terrible back problems and cannot move or work and lives with her, lying on the sofa all day long. She is certainly the most talented in the kingdom, but gets zero recognition. We, the tailors and shoemakers, we know of her gifts, but does the king? Do the townsfolk? She walks among them like an ordinary being, shopping for tomatoes, and no one knows that the world she's seeing is about a thousand times more detailed than the world anyone else is looking at. When you see a tomato, like me, you probably see a very nice red orb with a green stem, fresh and delectable. When she sees a tomato, she sees blues and browns, curves and indentations, shadow and light, and she could probably even guess how many seeds are in a given tomato based on how heavy it feels in her hand.

So we sent over the goat, and when the Color Master came into the studio, we'd just finished the fourth dyeing of the rock shoes. They were drying on a mat, and they looked pretty good. I told Cheryl that her visualization of the mountain had definitely helped. She blushed. I said, too, that Edwin's contribution of the ground rock particles had added a useful kind of rough texture. He kicked a stool leg, pleased. I hadn't done much; I'm not very skilled, but I like to commend good work when I see it.

The Color Master approached, wearing a linen sheath woven with blue threadings. Her face hinting at gaunt. She greeted us all, and stood at the counter where the shoes were drip-drying.

Nice work, she said. Esther, who had fronted the dyeing process, curtsied.

We sprinkled rocks into the dye, she said.

A fine choice, said the Color Master.

Edwin did a little dance in place by his table. The goat settled on a pillow in the corner and began to eat the stuffing.

The Color Master rolled her shoulders a

few times, and when the shoes were dry, she laid her hands upon them. She lifted them to the sunlight. She picked up a rock and looked at it next to the shoes. She circled both inside different light rays. Then she went to the palette area and took out a handful of blue dust. We have about one hundred and fifty metal bins of this dust in a range of colors. The bins stand side by side, running the perimeter of the studio. They are narrow, so we can fit a whole lot of colors, and if someone brings in a new color, we hammer down a new bin and slide it into the spectrum, wherever it fits. One tailor found an amazing rich burgundy off in the driest part of the forest, on a series of leaves; I located, once, over by the reddish iron deposits near the lake, a type of dirt that was a deeper brown than soil. Someone else found a new blue in a desiccated pansy, and another in the feathers of a dead bird. We have instructions to hunt for color everywhere, at all times.

The Color Master toured the room, and then took that handful of blue dust (and always, when I watch, I am thrilled — blue? how does she know, blue?), and she rubbed the dust into the shoe. Back to the bins, where she got a black, a dusty black, and then some sage green. While she worked, everyone stood around, quiet. We dropped our usual drudgery and chitchat.

The Color Master worked swiftly, but she added, usually, something on the level of forty colors, so the process generally took over two hours. She added a color here, a color there, sometimes at the size of salt particles, and the gray in the shoe shifted and shaded under her hands. She would reach a level and ask for sealant, and Esther would step forward, and the Color Master would coat the shoe to fasten the colors and then return to the sunlight, holding a shoe up, with the rock in her other hand. This went on for about four rounds. I swear, I could start to feel the original mountain's presence in the room, hear the great heavy lumbering voice of it.

When she was done, the pair was so gray, so rocklike, you could hardly believe they were made of leather at all. They looked as if they had been sheared straight from the craggy mountainside.

Done, she said.

We circled her, bowing our heads.

Another triumph, murmured Sandy, who cannot color-mix to save her life.

The Color Master swept her gaze around the room, and her eyes rested on each of us, searching, slowly, until they finally settled on me. Me?

Will you walk me home? she said in a deep voice, while Esther tied an invoice to the foot of a pigeon and then threw it out the window in the direction of the dukedom.

I would be honored, I mumbled. I took her arm. The goat, full of pillow, tripped along behind us.

I am a quiet sort, except for the paying of compliments, and I didn't know if I should ask her anything on the walk. As far as I knew, she didn't usually request an escort home at all. Mainly I just looked at all the stones and rocks on the path, and for the first time saw that blue hint, and the blackness, and the shades of green, and that faint edge of purple if the light hit just so. She seemed relieved that I wasn't asking questions, so much so that it occurred to me that that was probably why she'd asked me in the first place.

At her door, she fixed her eyes on me: steady, aging at the corners. She was almost twice my age, but had always had an allure I'd admired. A way of holding her body that let you know that there was a body there, but that it was private, that stuff happened on it, in it, to it, but it was stuff I would never see. It made me sad, seeing that, knowing how her husband had gone off to the war years ago and never returned, and how it was difficult for her to have people over because of her brother with the bad back, and how, long ago, she had fled her own town for reasons she never mentioned. Plus, she had a thick cough and her own money questions, all of which seemed so unfair when she should've been living in the palace, as far as I was concerned.

Listen, she said. She held me in her gaze.

Yes?

There's a big request coming in, she said. I've heard rumors. Big. Huge.

What is it? I said.

I don't know yet, but start preparing. You'll have to take over. I will die soon, she said.

Excuse me?

Soon, she said. I can feel it, brewing. Death. It's not dark, nor is it white. It's almost a blue-purple. Her eyes went past me, to the sky.

Are you confusing me with someone else? I asked.

She laughed.

Do you mean it? I said. Are you ill?

No, she said. Yes. I mean it. I'm asking for your help. And when I die, it will be your job to finish.

But I'm not very good, I said, twisting.

Like at all. You can't die. You should ask Esther, or Sven —

You, she said, and with a little curt nod, she went into her house and shut the door.

The duke loved his shoes so much he sent us a drawing, by the court illustrator, of him floating, it appeared, on a pile of rocks. I love them, he wrote, in swirly handwriting; I love them, I love them! In addition to a small cash bonus, he offered us horse rides and a feast at the dukedom. We all attended, in all our finery, and it was a great time. It was the last time I saw the Color Master dancing, in her pearl-gray gown, and I knew it was the last even as I watched it, her silver hair swirling out as she glided through the group. The duke kept tapping his toe on the side, holding the duchess's hand, her free one grasping a handbag the perfect pink of a rose, so vivid and fresh the color seemed to carry a sweet scent even across the ballroom.

Two weeks later, almost everyone was away when the king's courtier came riding over with the request: a dress the color of the moon. The Color Master was not feeling well, and had asked not to be disturbed; Esther's father was ill, so she was off taking care of him; Sven's wife was giving birth to twins, so he was off with her; the two others ahead of me had caught whooping cough; and someone else was on a travel trip to find a new orange. So the request went to me, the apprentice. Just as the Color Master had hoped.

I unrolled the scroll and read it quietly by the window.

A dress the color of the moon?

It was impossible.

First of all, the moon is not a color. It is a reflection of a color. Second, it is not even the reflection of a color. It is the reflection of what appears to be a color, but is really in fact a bunch of bursting hydrogen atoms, far, far away. Third, the moon shines. A dress cannot shine like the moon unless the dress is also reflecting something, and reflective materials are generally tacky-looking, or too industrial. Our only options were silk and cotton and leather. The moon? It is white, it is silver, it is silver-white, it is not an easy color to dye. A dress the color of the moon? The whole thing made me irritable.

But this was not a small order. This was, in fact, for the king's daughter. The princess. And since the queen had died of pneumonia a few months before, this was a dress for the most important woman in the kingdom.

I paced several times around the studio, and then I went against policy and tried knocking on the door of the Color Master's cabin, but she called out in a strong voice, Just make it!

Are you okay? I asked, and she said, Come back once you've started!

I walked back, kicking twigs and acorns.

I ate oranges off the tree out back until I felt a little better.

Since I was in charge, due to the pecking order, I called together everyone that was left in the studio and asked for a seminar on reflection, to reflect upon reflection. In particular for Cheryl, who really used the seminars well. We gathered in a circle in the side room and talked about mirrors, and still water, and wells, and feeling understood, and opals, and then we did a creative-writing exercise about our first memory of the moon, and how it affected us, and the moment when we realized it followed us (Sandy had a charming story about going on a walk as a child and trying to lose it but not being able to), and then we wrote haiku. Mine was this: Moon, you silver thing / Floating in the sky like that / Make me a dress. Please.

After a few tears over Edwin's story of realizing his father in the army was seeing the same moon he saw, we drifted out of the seminar room and began dyeing the silk. It had to be silk, of course, and we selected from the loom studio a very fine weave, a really elegant one that had a touch of shimmer in the fabric already. I let Cheryl start the dyeing with shades of white, because I could see a kind of shining light in her eyes from the seminar and even a luminosity to her skin. She is so receptive that way.

While she began that first layer, I went to see the Color Master again. I let myself in this time. She was in bed. It was shocking how quickly she was going downhill. I got her brother a glass of water and an apple-cheese snack — Angel, he called me, from the sofa — and then I settled next to the bed where she lay resting, her hair spread over the pillows in rays of silver. She was not very old, the Color Master, but she had gone silver early. Wait, can we use your hair? I said.

Sure. She pulled out a few strands and handed them over.

This'll help, I said, looking at the glint. If we try to make this into particles?

Good, she said. Good thinking.

How are you doing? I asked.

I heard word, she said. Moon today, sun soon.

What?

Sun soon. How goes moon?

It's hard, I said. I mean, *hard.* And, with your hair, that'll help, but to reflect?

Use blue, she said.

What kind?

Several kinds. Her voice was weaker, but I could hear the steel behind it as she walked through the bins in her mind. Don't be afraid of the darker shades, she said.

I'm an awful color-mixer, I said. Are you in pain?

No, she said. Just weak. Blue, she said. And black. She pulled out a few more strands of hair. Here, she said. And shavings of opal, do we have those?

Too expensive, I said.

Go to the mine, she said. Get opals, shave 'em, add a new bin. Do you know the king wants to marry his daughter? Her eyes flashed, for a second, with anger.

What?

Put that in the dress too, she said. She dropped her voice to a whisper, every word sharp and clear. Anger, she said. Put anger in the dress. The moon as our guide. A daughter should not be ordered to marry her father.

Put anger in the dress?

When you mix, she said. Got it? When

you're putting the opal shavings in. The dress is supposed to be a dowry gift, but give the daughter the strength to leave instead. All right?

Her eyes were shining at me, so bright I wanted to put them in the dress, too.

Okay, I said, faltering. I'm not sure —

You have it in you, she said. I see it. Truly. Or I would never have given you the job.

Then she fell back on her pillows and was asleep in seconds.

On the walk back, through the scrub-oak grove, I felt as I usually felt, both moved and shitty. Because what she saw in me could just as easily have been the result of some kind of fever. Was she hallucinating? Didn't she realize I had only gotten the job because I'd complimented Esther on her tassel scarf at the faire, plus I did decent work with the rotating time schedule? Who's to say that there was anything to it? To me, really?

Anger in the dress?

I didn't feel angry, just defeated and bad about myself, but I didn't put that in the dress; it didn't seem right. Instead, I went to the mine and befriended the foreman, Manny, and he gave me a handful of opals that were too small for any jewelry and would work well as shavings. I spent the afternoon with the sharpest picks and awls I could find, breaking open opals and making a new bin for the dust. Cheryl had done wonders with the white, and the dress glowed like a gleaming pearl — almost moonlike but not enough, yet. I added the opals and we redyed, and then you could see a hint of rainbow hovering below the surface. Like the sun was shimmering in there, too, and that was addressing the reflective issue. When it came time to color-mix, I felt like I was going to throw up, but I did what the Color Master had asked, and went for blue, then black, and I was incredibly slow, like incredibly slow, but for one moment I felt something as I hovered over the bins of blue. Just a tug of guidance from the white of the dress that led my hand to the middle blue. It felt, for a second, like harmonizing in a choir, the moment when the voice sinks into the chord structure and the sound grows, becomes more layered and full than before. So that was the right choice. I wasn't so on the mark for the black, which was slightly too light, more like the moon when it's just setting, when the light of day has already started to rise and encroach, which isn't what they wanted — they wanted black-of-night moon, of course.

But when we held it up in the middle of the room, there it was — not as good as anything the Color Master had done, maybe one one-hundredth as good, but there was something in it that would pass the test of the assignment. Like, the king and princess wouldn't collapse in awe, but they would be pleased, maybe even a little stirred. Color is nothing unless next to other colors, the Color Master told us all the time. Color does not exist alone. And I got it, for a second with that blue, I did.

Cheryl and I packed the dress carefully in a box, and sent off the pigeon with the invoice, and waited for the king's courtiers to come by, and they did, with a carriage for the dress only. After we laid the box carefully on the velvet backseat, they gave us a hunk of chocolate as a bonus, which Cheryl and I ate together in the side room, exhausted. Relieved. I went home and slept for twenty hours. I had put no anger in the dress; I remembered that when I woke up. Who can do that while so focused on just making an acceptable moon-feeling for the assignment? They didn't ask for anger, I said, eating a few apples for breakfast. They asked for the moon, and I gave them something vaguely moonlike, I said, spitting tooth cleanser into the basin.

That afternoon, I went to see the Color Master to tell her all about it. I left out the absence of the anger and told her I'd messed up on the black, and she laughed and laughed from her bed. I told her about the moon being more of a morning moon. I told her what I'd felt at the blue, the feeling of the chord, and she picked up my hand. Pressed it lightly.

Death is glowing, she said. I can see it.

I felt a heaviness rustle in my chest. How long? I said.

A few weeks, I think, she said. The sun will come in soon. The princess still has not left the castle.

But we need you, I said, and with effort, she squeezed my hand again. It is dark and glowing, she said, her eyes sliding over to lock onto mine. It is like loam, she said.

The sun? I said.

Tomorrow, she said. She closed her eyes.

When I got to work the next day, there was an elaborate thank-you note from the castle with a lot of praise for the moon dress, in this over-the-top calligraphy, and a bonus bolt of fuchsia silk. The absentees were returning, slowly, from their various tangents, when we received the king's new assignment: a dress the color of the sun. Because everyone felt a little jittery about

242

the Color Master's absence and wanted to go with whatever — or whoever — seemed to work, I was assigned to the order. Esther told me congratulations. Sandy took over my rotating schedule duties. I did a few deep knee bends and got to work.

I liked that guy at the mine a little bit, the Manny guy, so I went back to ask about citrine quartz. He didn't have any, but we had a nice roast-turkey lunch together in the spot of sun outside the rocky opening of the cave, and I told him about the latest dress I was making for the princess.

Whew, he said, shaking his head. What color *is* the sun?

Beats me, I said. We're not supposed to look at it, right? Kids make it yellow, I said, but I think that's not quite right.

Ivory? he said.

Sort of burnt white, I said. But with a halo?

That's hard work, he said, folding up the cloth he used to hold his sandwich. He had a good face to him, something chunky in his nose that I could get behind.

Want to go to the faire sometime? he asked, looking up.

The outdoor faire happened on the week-ends in the main square, where everything was sold.

Sure, I said.

Maybe there's some sun stuff there, he said.

I'd love to, I said.

We began the first round of dyeing at the end of the week, focusing initially on the pale yellows. Cheryl was very careful not to oversaturate the dye — yellow is always more powerful than it appears in the bin. It is a stealth dominator, and can take days and days to undo. She did that all Saturday, while I went to the faire. It was a clear, warm afternoon, with stands offering all sorts of goodies and delicious meat pies. Nothing looked helpful for the dress, but Manny and I laughed about the latest tapestry unicorn craze and shared a nice kiss at the end, near the scrub oaks. Everything was feeling a little more alive than usual. We held another seminar at the studio, and Cheryl did a session on warmth, and seasons, and how we all revolve around the sun, whether or not we are willing to admit it. Central, she said. The theme of the sun is central. The center of us, she said. Core. Fire.

Careful with red, said the Color Master, when I went to visit. She was thinner and weaker, but her eyes were still coals. Her brother had gotten up to try to take care of her and had thrown out his back to the worst degree and was now in the medicine arena, strapped to a board. My sister is dying, he told the doctors, but he couldn't move, so all they did was shake their heads. The Color Master had refused any help. I want to see Death as clearly as possible, she'd said. No drugs.

I made her some toast, but she only ate a few bites and then pushed it aside.

It's tempting to think of red for sun, she said. But it has to be just a dash, not much. More of a dark orange, and a hint of brown. And then white on yellow on white.

Not bright white, she said. The kind of white that makes you squint, but in a softer way.

Yeah, I said, sighing. And where does one find that kind of white?

Keep looking, she said.

Last time I used your hair? I said.

She smiled, feebly. Go look at fire for a while, she said. Go spend some time with fire.

I don't want you to die, I said.

Yes, well, she said. And?

Looking at fire was interesting, I have to

admit. I sat with a candle for a couple hours. It has these stages of color: the white, the yellow, the red, the tiny spot of blue I'd heard mentioned but never noticed. So I decided it made sense to use all of them. We hung the dress in the center of the room and all revolved around it, spinning, imagining we were planets. It needs to be hotter, said Sven, who was playing the part of Mercury, and then he put a blowtorch to some silk and made some dust materials out of that, and we redipped the dress. Cheryl was off in the corner, cross-legged in a sunbeam, her eyes closed, trying to soak it up. We need to soak it! she said, after an hour, standing. So we left it in the dipping longer than usual. I walked by the bins, trying to feel that harmony feeling, waiting for a color to call me. I felt a tug to the dark brown, so I brought a bit of it out and tossed it into the mix; it was too dark, but after a little yellow-white from dried lily flowers, something started to pop a bit. Light, said Cheryl. It's also daylight — it's light. It's our only true light, she said again. Without it, we live in darkness and cold. The dress drip-dried in the middle of the room. It was getting closer, and just needed that factor of squinting — a dress so bright it couldn't quite be looked at.

How to get that?

Remember, the Color Master said. She sat up in bed, her silver hair streaming over her shoulders. I keep forgetting, she said, but the king wants to Marry His Daughter. Her voice pointed to each word, hard. That is not right, she said, okay? Got it? Put anger in the dress. Righteous anger, for her. Do you hear me?

I do not, I said, though I nodded. I didn't say I do not, I just thought that part. I played with the wooden knob of her bedframe. I had tried to put some anger in the sun dress, but I had been so consumed with trying to factor in the squint that all I really got in there was confusion. Confusion does make people squint, though, so I ended up fulfilling the request accidentally. We had sent it off in the carriage after working all night on the light factor that Cheryl had mentioned by adding bits of diamond dust to the mix. Diamonds are light inside darkness! she'd announced at 3 a.m., a bialy in her hand, triumphant. On the whole, it was a weaker product than the moon dress, but not bad — most people don't notice the variance in subtlety, and our level of general artistry and craft is high, so we could get away with a lot without anyone's running over and asking for his money back.

The sky, the Color Master told me, after I had filled her in on the latest. She had fallen back down into her pillows, and was so weak she spoke with eyes closed. When I held her hand she only rested hers in mine: not limp, not grasping.

Sky is last, she said.

And death?

Soon, she said. She fell asleep midway through our conversation. I stayed all night. I slept too, sitting up, and sometimes I woke and just sat and watched her. What a precious person she was, really. I hadn't known her very well, but she had picked me, for some reason, and that picking was changing me, I could feel it; it was like being warmed by the presence of the sun, a little. The way a ray of sun can seem to choose you as you walk outside from the cold interior. I wanted to put her in that sun dress, to drape her in it, but it wasn't an option; we had sent it off to the princess, plus it wasn't even the right size and wasn't really her style, either. But I guess I just knew that the sun dress we sent was something of a facsimile, and that this person here was the real sun, the real center for us all, and even through the dark night, I felt the light of her, burning, even in the rasping heavy breathing of a dying woman.

In the morning, she woke up, saw I was still there, and smiled a little. I brought her tea. She sat up to drink it.

The anger! she said again, as if she had been dreaming about it. Which maybe she had. She raised up on her elbows, face blazing. Don't forget to put anger in this last dress, she said. Okay?

Drink your tea, I said.

Listen, she said. It's important, she said. She shook her head. It was written, in pain, all over her forehead. She sat up higher on her elbows, and looked beyond me, through me, and I could feel meaning, thick, in her, even if I didn't know the details about why. She picked her words carefully.

You cannot bring it — someone — into the world, and then bring it back into you, she said. It is the wrong action.

Her face was clear of emphasis, and she spoke plainly, as plainly as possible, as if there were no taboo about fathers marrying daughters, as if the sex factor was not a biological risk, as if it wasn't just disturbing and upsetting as a given. She held herself steady on her elbows. This is why she was the Color Master. There was no stigma, or judgment, no societal subscription, no trigger morality, but just a clean and pure anger, fresh, as if she was thinking the possibility over for the first time.

You birth someone, she said, leaning in. And then you release her. You do not marry her, which is a bringing back in. You let her go.

Put anger in the dress, she said. She gripped my hand, and suddenly all the weakness was gone, and she was right there, an electric pulse of a person, and I knew this was the last time we would talk, I knew it so clearly that everything sharpened into incredible focus. I could see the threads in the weave of her nightgown, the microscopic bright cells in the whites of her eyes.

Her nails bit into my hand. I felt the tears rising up in me. The teacup wobbling on the nightstand.

Got it? she said.

Yes, I said.

I put the anger in the dress the color of sky. I put it in there so much I could hardly stand it — that she was about to die, that she would die unrecognized, that none of us would ever live up to her example, and that we were the only witnesses. That we are all so small after all that. That everybody dies anyway. I put the anger in there so much that the blue of the sky was fiercely stark, an electric blue like the core of the fire, so much that it was hard to look at. It was much harder to look at than the sun dress; the sky dress was of a whole different order. Intensely, shockingly, bluely vivid. Let her go? This was the righteous anger she had asked for, yards of it, bolts of it, even though, paradoxically, it was anger I felt because soon she would be gone.

She died the following morning in her sleep. Even at her funeral, all I could feel was the rage, pouring out of me, while we all stood around her coffin, crying, leaning on one another, sprinkling colors from the dye bins into her hands, the colors of heaven, we hoped, while the rest of the town went about its business. Her brother rolled in on a stretcher, weeping. I had gone over to see her that morning, and found her, dead, in her bed. So quiet. The morning sun, white and clear, through the window-panes. I stroked her hair for an hour, her silver hair, before I left to tell anyone. The dress request had already come in the day before, as predicted.

At the studio, under deadline, Cheryl led a seminar on blue, and sky, and space, and atmosphere, and depth, and it was success-ful and mournful, especially during the week after the funeral. Blue. I attended, but mostly I was nurturing the feeling in me, that rage. Tending to it like a little candle flame cupped against the wind. I knew it was the right kind, I knew it. I didn't think I'd do much better than this dress, ever; I would go on to do good things in my life, have other meaningful moments, share in the experience of being a human being in the world, but I knew this was my big moment, and I had to be equal to it. So I sat at the seminar with half a focus, just cupping that flame of rage, and I half participated in the dyeing of the fabric and the discussion of the various shades, and then, when they had done all they could do, and the dress was hanging in the middle, a clear and beautiful blue, I sent everyone home. Are you sure? Cheryl asked, buttoning up her coat.

Yes, I said. Go.

It was night, and the sky was unlit under a new moon, so it was up to me to find the blue sky — draped over us all, but hidden. I went to the bins, and listened for the chords, and felt her in me. I felt the ghost of her passing through me as I mixed and dyed, and I felt the rage in me that she had to be a ghost: the softness of the ghost, right up next to and surrounding the sharp and burning core of my anger. Both guided my hands. I picked the right colors to mix with blue, a little of so many other colors and then so many different kinds of blue and gray and more blue and more. And in it all, the sensation of shaking my fists at the sky, shaking my fists high up to the sky, because that is what we do when someone dies too early, too beautiful, too undervalued by the world, or sometimes just at all — we shake our fists at the big blue beautiful indifferent sky, and the anger is righteous and strong and helpless and huge. I shook and I shook, and I put all of it into the dress.

Of all people to take back? How impossible to understand that I would never see her again.

When the sun rose, it was a clear morning, the early sky pale and wide. I had worked all night. I wasn't tired yet, but I could feel the pricklings of it around me, peripheral. I made a pot of coffee and sat in the chill with a cup and the dress, which I had hung again from a hanger in the middle of the room. The rest of the tailors drifted over in the morning, one by one, and no one said anything. They entered the room and looked up, and then they surrounded it with me. We held hands, and they said I was the new Color Master, and I said okay, because it was obvious that that was true, and though

I knew I would never reach her levels again, at least for this one dress I had. They didn't even praise me, they just looked at it and cried. We all cried.

Esther sent off the invoice pigeon, and, with care, we placed the dress in its package, and when the carriage came by, we laid it carefully over the backseat, as usual. We ate our hunk of gift chocolate. We cleaned up the area around the bins and swept the floor of dust, and talked to a builder, a friend of Manny's, about expanding one of the rooms into an official seminar studio. The carriage trotted off, with the dress in the backseat, led by two white horses.

From what I heard, soon after the princess got the third dress, she left town. The rest I do not know.

The rest of the story — known, I'm told, as "Donkeyskin" — is hers.

A State of Variance

On her fortieth birthday, the woman lost the ability to sleep for more than a single hour. She did not accumulate a tired feeling; in fact, that one hour served the purpose of eight, and she awoke refreshed. But because that hour was full of only the most intense, involving sleep, the sleep beyond rapid eye movement, the consequence was that she had no time in her sleep hours for dreams. So, during the day, she would experience moments when the rules of the world would shift and she would see, inside her teakettle, a frog floating, dead. And then blink and it would be gone. Or she would greet the mailman and he would hand her a basket of seawater, dripping, with stamps floating wetly on top. And then she would smile and bring in the mail. These moments sprinkled throughout every day; she still had a driver's license and wondered if she should revoke it herself, as the zombies who passed through the crosswalk and disappeared into the lamppost were confusing.

She assumed she would die at eighty. She figured this because the sleep shift began on her fortieth birthday and all her life, things had happened symmetrically like that. Her birthdate was 11.25.52, and that was not notable until she realized that she had been born in Amsterdam and there the day comes first: 25.11.52; the address of the only house she could afford for miles and miles was 1441, on a street named Circle Road on the edges of Berkeley. She had a son the day her father died. Her son's face was almost a perfect mirror of itself, in such a way that one realized how imperfections created trust, because no one trusted her son with that perfect symmetry in his face; contrary to the magazine articles that stated that women would orgasm easily above him, beneath him, due to that symmetry, no — his symmetry was too much, and women shied away, certain he was a player. Certain he would dump them. And because no one approached him, when he did have girlfriends every now and again he *would* dump them, because he found he did not trust them either, because they were always looking at him so furtively — making, with their faces, the action of holding up your hands in front of your chest to block a blow.

He told his mother he could not seem to meet a woman who had a core strength to her, and his mother, studying geometry at the kitchen table with cutouts of triangles and squares, said she was sorry for what her pregnancy had done.

"What did it do?" he asked.

She held a mirror up to his nose. He saw his face in the hinged reflection. "What?" he said. Then she did it to herself, and the sight of his mother in perfect matched halves so disturbed him that he went and made himself a huge ham sandwich.

"So what are you saying?" he asked, mouth full of meat.

"I am saying that your face repels trust," she said. "Because it is too exact. I am saying," she told him, "that I will die on my eightieth birthday, because I stopped sleeping at forty."

He knew, in a vague way, about the sleeping. The shapes on the table danced in front of her and slipped into her mouth, large mints. Then they were regular again. The mirror on the table was a mouth. She put a finger in and it bit her, wet. She'd finally told her son about the sleeping when he complained that she had made him too many colorful crocheted blankets and he had no more room for them in his apartment. "Take them to the shelter," he'd pleaded, and then asked, "How are you making all these anyway? Are you taking drugs?" (He himself had been taking overdoses of B vitamins to relieve stress to take the edge off how he felt when he smiled at another person who seemed to have an inordinately tough time smiling back.) His mother had laughed. She told him not about the dreaming aspect but about the one hour, the way she didn't feel tired, and how it began promptly on her fortieth birthday.

He finished his sandwich and touched the blob of mustard left on the plate with the tip of his finger.

"Are you saying you believe in some kind of grand plan?" he asked. "Because I never thought you raised me to believe in any kind of overarching concept."

"I'm just noticing the patterns," she said. But her voice was so doubtful that he made a mental note with the sponge in his hand to be sure to be there on that eightieth birthday itself, so that she would not try to do anything herself, so interested in the pattern that she might let herself be a sacrifice to it.

Neither missed their father/husband, who

traveled so often he was unrecognizable when he returned. He came back from the latest trip with his hair dyed black and a deadly cough that landed him in the hospital. He lay there for weeks and weeks, and his hair grew in long and brown. The cough got worse. Above him, before death, stood his symmetrical son, whom even he did not trust, and his wife, whom he could not sleep next to anymore, as she read until all hours and wanted to talk to him and had forgotten that other people needed more than an hour. She resented the world, he felt, resented that all people were not exactly like her in this way. She was so lonely for those seven hours, and when he awoke he always felt that she was slightly blaming him for sleeping. After she had turned forty, he traveled more, for years, so that those eight hours could be his alone, and in different cities he loved different beds — his mistresses not flesh and blood but made of pillows and sheets and the wide-open feeling of waking up without alarm or expectation. As he died, as he looked at these two people he loved most, he only thought: What a curious pair they are, aren't they? And then it was the white light, and he felt fine about succumbing to it. He was not, by nature, a big fighter.

A year or so after his father died, the son felt a strong desire to get his mother a suitor, so that she would not lean on him as the main man in her life. He knew a son's role could be confused that way, just as he'd felt the tugging from inside all those crocheted blankets, and he was too keenly vulnerable himself to the attention. He could see it, marriage to Mom, never official or blessed, and yet as implicit as breakfast or dinner. He did not want that. For all the lack of trust the world had bestowed upon him, he still had hope that something would happen to his face that would soften its appearance to others, and allow him into the palm of true love. So he went on a dating search for his mother. He answered several personal ads on Craigslist for men who were looking for women that sounded, more or less, like her, and so he wrote them, explaining that he was looking for his mother, and invited them, one by one, over to the house on 1441 Circle Road, under the guise of landscape gardener. The men were skeptical about the idea, which seemed untrustworthy, and even more skeptical once they met the kid, who seemed untrustworthy, but they all fell for his mother, almost elegantly, and in contrast to the general lore that good men were difficult to find, here were four, almost instantly, who were ready to take her mourning and knead it into their hearts. Two became her weekend companions: one on Sunday day, one on Friday evening. She did not tell them of the sleeping, or of how, when she was watching a movie, another movie often superimposed itself onto the screen, so that when he asked, after, how she'd liked it, she wasn't sure which movie he had seen and which was her dream addition.

The son now had some space to do things. His father was gone. Which was sad, but his father had never trusted him, and that had always been a problem. He went to the Grind It Up coffee shop down the street from his apartment in Oakland and ordered himself a raisin scone and a black tea. Then he sat down at the table of a large man, a man with tattoos but the old kind, before tattoos became dainty and about spiritual life. This man wore tattoos from the time when tattoos meant you liked to kick people around.

"Yes?" the man said, moving his newspaper aside.

The young man didn't move. He sipped his tea.

"I'm sitting here?" said the man. He was a

big man too. He took up most of the table. There were plenty of other free tables in the café. The young man trembled inside, but he kept his hand steady. He steadied his symmetrical face.

"You a homo or something?" asked the man.

The son didn't respond. But he could see the man digesting the face, the perfect face, and the man lifted the table gently, and the scone slid down into the boy's lap, and the tea wobbled, and the boy just put the scone back on the now slanted table and kept his eyes on the scrawny facial hair of the man.

The man, Marty, was tired. He did not want to fight. He had done that so many times before. He was tired of it, and he was taking classes now, and they told him to acknowledge how he was really hurt inside, not angry at all. He read his paper high over his head and stopped looking at the young man. So it was a homo. So he was picked up today at the café by a homo. This was new for him. He decided to do what that lady said, and try to find the humor in it, and when he did he really did find it funny, and behind his paper, he started to laugh.

Well, the young man was stuck. He'd wanted a hit, a real hit, a hit that would complicate his face. Finally he put a hand on the man's newspaper, folding it down. "Listen," he said. "I'm sorry to bother you, but I just want to get hit." Marty laughed and laughed some more. His arm tattoo read *Skull Keeper,* and had an illustration of bones wrapped in ribbons. "You want to get hit?" he said. "Too bad. I'm done with that shit."

"Please?" said the young man, and Marty said no, but the tight businessman eavesdropping at the next table with an iced mocha blend said he'd do it, sure, a hit?

"Right on the cheek," said the young man, and he asked Marty to oversee, because now he trusted Marty far more than the tight businessman, whose smile was far too pleased at the idea. "Let's all go out back? Please?" he asked Marty, who folded up his paper and agreed, because it was the modern world, and he was old but open-minded, and being the protector was a better role for him anyway, maybe a role to consider, in fact, for the future. And the tight businessman looked so tightly delighted, and the boy said, "Cheek, please," but he did not know the tight businessman had poor centering perception, and had never, in fact, hit another man, although he'd wanted to, his whole life, ever since he had been teased every day on the walk to school by that bastard boy Adam Vermouth, who had told him in a squawking voice that he was useless, useless, useless. The tight businessman played with his hands as fists all the time at the office, but when put in the actual situation, aiming for the cheek, what he got instead was the nose, and he slammed the boy straight on and broke the bone, blood pouring out of his nostrils. "Okay?" said Marty, holding his arms out flat like a referee. "Are we done?" "That's good," gasped the boy, reeling with pain, and the tight businessman was just warming up, was dancing on his toes, ready to pummel this handsome young man into the brick of the café's back wall, but Marty clamped one soft big paw on the businessman's shoulder and said, "You're done now, son." The tight businessman relaxed under Marty's hand, and the young man, too, relaxed under Marty's voice, and later, Marty did decide that it had been a far better day for him, being the fight mediator, the protective bulldog, and when he told the lady he had figured something out, tears broke into his eyes, like eggs cracking, bright and fresh. She was proud of him. He was such a good man inside, underneath all the butt kicking and bravado.

The young man, bleeding all over the wall,

waved off offers to go to the hospital or the doctor. "No, thank you, thank you," he said, stumbling inside, using up a pile of brown recycled napkins, then holding the café's one pint of coffee ice cream to his nose, and the businessman kept saying, "It will heal poorly," and the young man said that was the point. And he shook the hand of the tight businessman, who was feeling cheated, as if he'd had a taste of nectar he could hardly even feel in his mouth. The young man waved at Marty, who was at the pay phone telling about his revelation, and he headed home. There, he tended to his nose for days, hoping and hoping, and he went over to his mother's on the day he was ready to really look at it straight on, ready to remove the Band-Aids making a little pattern all over his face. She was in the kitchen, eating jelly beans off the counter — eating them even when they turned into tiny tractors and then back again — and she helped him peel each Band-Aid off, one at a time, and then they both went to the bathroom mirror. She put a hand on his shoulder. They stared at his face for a long, long time.

What had happened of course is that it had healed symmetrically. The nose was severely broken and bumpy, but the bump was a band over the middle of his nose. It had complicated the vertical planes of his face, but horizontally he still matched himself exactly. The young man's eyes filled, and he felt the despair rushing into his throat, but his mother, wiping his cheeks clear of the leftover crusted blood, breath smelling of jelly beans, listened to the story and laughed, and said, "Son, my sweet, sweet son, it's just that you are a butterfly. That's just what you are. I don't think you can do anything about it."

Finally, he was eating a hamburger one afternoon and, licking the ketchup off the knife, he cut open the side of his lip. It was a small mark, but it needed stitches, and when they took out the stitches he had a small raised area above the left side of his lip which provided the desperately needed window. He met a woman — Sherrie-Marla — in a week. True, about a month or two later, she, while kissing him passionately, bit the other side, creating an identical mark. She dabbed ice on his lip, apologizing, and he dreaded it, dreaded her change, his eyes filling with tears in advance of her leaving, but the fact was, Sherrie-Marla trusted him already. When he took the ice off, and showed to her his new symmetry, she didn't flinch. His face was him to her now; it was not a map or an indicator of some abstract idea. Turned out it was only the first impression he'd needed to alter.

His mother came over for brunch with her Sunday suitor, and when she saw Sherrie-Marla take her son's hand and kiss it on the thumb, a circle completed inside her.

In bed, after the brunch, Sherrie-Marla turned to him with clear eyes, touching his lip wound with her fingertips, her head propped on her open hand.

"You have movie star lips now," Sherrie-Marla told him, smiling, as he leaned in to kiss her, tenderly, her kisses very, very gentle on the sore area, just pillows in the air between them.

Her own face was wildly asymmetrical. One eye much higher than the other. A nostril tilted. The smile lopsided. The front right tooth chipped. The dented chin. The larger right breast. The slightly gnarled foot. It had caused her her own share of problems. We are all, generally, symmetrical: ants, elephants, lions, fish, flowers, leaves. But she was a tree. No one expects a tree to be symmetrical at all. It opens its arms, in its unevenness, and he, the butterfly, flew inside.

When we came home from the movie that night, my sister went into the bathroom and then called out to our mother, asking if she'd bought another toothpaste as a hint.

I know I have major cavities, she said. But do we really need two?

Two what? asked my mother.

Two toothpastes, said Hannah.

My mother took off her jacket for the first time in hours, and peered in the bathroom, where, next to the grungy blue cup that holds the toothbrushes, there were now two full toothpastes.

I only bought one, she said. I think. Unless for some reason it was on sale.

We all shrugged in unison. I brushed my teeth with extra paste and went to bed. This incident would've been filed away in non-memory and we would just have had clean teeth for longer, except that in the morning there was a new knickknack on the living room side table, a slim abstract circle made of silver, and no one had any idea where it came from.

Is it a present? asked our mother with motherly hope, but we children, all too honest, shook our heads.

I don't know what that is, I said, picking it up. It felt heavy, and expensive. Cool to the touch. Nice, Hannah said.

My mother put it away in the top of the coat closet. It was nice, but it felt, she said, like charity. And I don't like too many knickknacks, she said, eyes elsewhere, wondering. She went to my grandmother and brought her a lukewarm cup of tea, which Grandma accepted and held, as if she no longer knew what to do with it.

Drink! my mother said, and Grandma took a sip and the peppermint pleased her and she smiled.

Happened again the next evening when, while setting up for a rare family dinner, my mother stood, arms crossed, in front of the pantry.

Lisa, she said, you didn't go to the market, did you?

Me?

Hannah?

No.

John?

No.

Grandma never shopped. She would get lost in the aisles. She would hide beneath the apple table like a little girl. Our mother, mouth twisted to the side in puzzlement, found soup flavors in the pantry she swore she never would've considered buying. She held up a can of lobster bisque. This is far too bourgeois for me, she said. Wild rice and kidney bean? she said. Lemongrass corn chowder?

Yum, yelled Dad from the other room, where he was watching tennis.

Hannah paused, placing spoons on napkins. I don't really like soup, she said. I shook my head. Not me, I said. I definitely hate soup.

Our mother tapped her fingers against the counter. What is going on? she asked.

Hannah lined up the spoon with the knife. We've been backwards robbed, she said solemnly.

I laughed, but her eyes were serious.

All's I know is, she said, I did not buy that soup.

Neither did I, said Mom.

Neither did I, called Dad from the other room.

I could tell I was still the main suspect, just because I seemed the most interested in all of it, but as I explained repeatedly, why would a person lie about bringing food and new knickknacks into the house? That is nice. That is something to get credit for.

Dad cooked up the corn chowder after he found an enormous piece of gristle in his mustard chicken. We all watched him closely for choking or poisoning, but he smiled after each spoonful and said it was darned good and very unusual. Like Southwestern Thai, he said, wiping his mouth. Like . . . the empress meets Kimosabe, he said. Like . . . silver meets turquoise, he said, laughing. Like . . . We all told him that was enough. Hannah checked the inside of the can for clues. After dinner, Dad collected water glasses from the rooms, singing.

That night, I kept a close eye on the back door, but it stayed locked; I even fixed a twig at its base to see if it got jigged during the night, but in the morning, all was just as before. I was walking to the bathroom to get ready for school when Mom cried out, and I ran over, and she was standing over the kitchen table, which held an extra folded newspaper. Hannah found a third pewter candlestick that matched the previous two, standing tall in the bookshelf. We ate our breakfasts in silence. Although getting robbed would be bad, there was nothing appealing about getting *more* items every day, and I felt a vague sense of claustrophobia pick up in my lungs, like I might get smothered under extra throw pillows in the middle of the night. And we couldn't even sell the new stuff for extra cash, because everything we got was just messed up enough to make it unappealing — the pewter candlestick was flaking into little slivers, and the silver circle thing had a subtle, creepy smell.

For the first time in my life, I cleaned my room after school. I threw out tons of old magazines and trash and dumb papers for school with the teacher's red pen stating: *Lisa, we all know you can do better than this.* While cleaning, I found a new mug on my side table, with a picture of dancing cows holding Happy Birthday balloons. It could only have been purchased by Hannah, but when I showed it to her she started to cry.

They're trying to kill us! she said, sobbing, wiping her nose on her T-shirt.

Who? How? How are they trying to kill us?

The people bringing this stuff in.

But who's bringing it in? I asked. We've been home the whole time.

Ghosts, she said, eyes huge. She stared at the mug. It's not even your birthday, she said, not for months and months.

I stuck the mug in the outside trash can, along with the extra newspaper. I kept my eyes on all the doors. The twig stayed put.

We had a respite for a week, and everyone calmed down a bit and my mother went to the market and counted how many cans, so she'd know. We ate the food we bought. We stared at the knickknacks that represented our personalities. All was getting back to normal until the next Sunday, when Hannah opened the towel closet and screamed at the top of her lungs.

What? We ran to her.

The towel closet had towels in it. Usually it had small thin piles — we each had a towel and were expected to use it over four days for all towel purposes, and there'd be a big towel wash twice a week, one on Thursday, one on Sunday. We never stuck to the system, and so generally I just used my towel as long as I possibly could, until the murky smell of mildew and toothpaste started to pass from it onto me, undoing all the cleaning work of the previous shower.

Now the towel closet was full, not of anything fluffy, but of more thin and ugly towels. Tons of them. At least ten more towels, making the piles high.

Well, I said. I guess we can cut the

Thursday-Sunday wash cycle.

My mother went off to breathe in a paper bag. Hannah straightened taller, and then put one towel around her hair and another around her body, a very foreign experience in our family.

I'm going to just appreciate the gifts, she said, even though her face looked scared. I've always wanted to use two at once, she said.

At school the next week, it was past Halloween and we had to bring in our extra candies for the poor children of Glendora. Bags and bags came pouring in, and aside from candy, I brought in an extra bag of stuff full of soup cans and knickknacks I'd salvaged from the trash. Everyone in the family felt funny about it; maybe it was like passing on something toxic. But at the same time, throwing out whole unopened cans of lobster soup struck my mother as obscene. How often does a homeless woman who lives nowhere near salt water get lobster? she asked, hands on hips, as I packed up the bag. We nodded. We liked how her guilt looked in this form of benevolence. I repeated it to my teacher. It's not a Snickers, I said, but it's got a lot more protein.

I believe I saw my teacher take that soup can for herself. I watched her closely that week, but she seemed fine, and my dad had never had a single negative symptom from his lemongrass corn chowder. I didn't eat any Halloween candy. I didn't want anything from anyone else.

I got a note from the shelter saying my bag was the best.

Hannah got a boyfriend. She didn't tell anyone, but I could tell because she was using so many towels, making the bathroom a pile of towels, and for some reason I knew the towels were happening because of a boy. Why did she need to be so dry all the time? I asked her about it, when she came home for dinner and looked all pretty with her cheeks bright like that. I had to set the table because she was late, and she apologized and said she'd take dish duty for two days.

It's okay, I said. Who is he?

She blushed, crazily. Who is who?

The reason you are late, I said.

I had to study.

Mom stood in the door frame, but she wasn't listening.

How was your math test? Mom said, brushing the side of her hair with a soup-spoon.

Okay, said Hannah, glaring at me. I got an A.

What did you hear? she asked, dragging

me aside and cutting into my arm with her budding nails.

Nothing, I said. Ow. I just guessed.

How? she said.

No reason, I said. Towels. Who is it?

She said no one, but then she barely ate at dinner, which is rare for her — usually I have to fight my way to the main dish to even get any, because she is so hungry — and that let me know she really liked him.

Dad lost his job. Then he got a new job. Then he got his old job back and went back to it. They were all in the same building.

We didn't get any more items for a few weeks. I started to miss them. I mean, I felt like I would die of claustrophobia and I had become paranoid about all things new coming into the house, including the bathwater exiting the faucet tap, and I had made a checklist for market items, shopping items, and all school items, but when I opened the refrigerator and saw all the same old stuff, I wanted to cry sometimes.

I left a few baits: I cleared my nightstand of all things, so that it was ready for a deposit. I bought a lobster soup with my own allowance, which made my mother shriek, but I assured her I'd bought it and I'd even saved the receipt to prove it. I brought it out of my bedroom, and she stared at the curling white paper and then looked at me, in the way she rarely did, eye to eye.

Are you okay, Lisa? she said. Ten-year-olds don't usually save receipts.

I'm trying to trap a ghost, I said.

Would you like to go to the mall? she asked. Her eyes were tired. She looked pretty with tired eyes, so I didn't mind so much.

We went to the nearest mall, over in Cerritos, which had been built twenty years ago and was ugly. I liked that about it. It was like a relative nobody liked but everybody still had to be related to anyway. We went to the kids' store and she bought me two shirts, one orange, one red, and then I got very attached to a particular cap with an octopus on the cap part, and I felt if I left it in the store I might dissolve. I didn't have much allowance left due to the spenditure of the lobster soup, and so I asked my mom as nicely as I could if I could have an advance and get the octopus cap because I loved it very much.

That? She was holding the store bag and trying to stop the salesperson from talking to her by staring out the door. Thanks, she was saying, thanks, thanks.

I love it, I said, putting it on my head. It

was too big. I couldn't see well underneath it.

Please? I said.

We just got you two new shirts, she said. Do you really need a cap?

It's good for skin cancer, I said. Of the face.

She laughed. She was tired these days because she was having job trouble too; her job trouble meant she did not know how she could be useful in her life. Dad's job trouble was he had too much to do with his life. Sometimes I just wanted them to even it out but I couldn't think of how. That afternoon, I didn't want to bother her more, but I wasn't certain I could leave the store with that cap still in it. If someone else bought it, I might tear in two.

I will pay you back, I said. I swear. Or we can exchange it for one of the shirts?

She got me the cap because I hardly ever asked for much, and at home I slept with it on, and wore my new orange shirt to school and back, and I was ready to charge ahead into my afternoon activities when I noticed the octopus cap on my dresser.

I thought it was the one on my head, except then I realized that that one was already on my head. So this had to be a new one? I took the one on my head off and held them both side by side. Two octopus caps. I had two now. One, two. They were both exactly the same, but I kept saying right hand, right hand, in my head, so I'd remember which one I'd bought, because that was the one I wanted. I didn't want another octopus cap. It was about this particular right-hand octopus cap; that was the one I had fallen in love with. Somehow, it made me feel so sad, to have two. So sad I thought I couldn't stand it.

I took the new one, left hand, to the trash, but then I thought my mom might see it and get mad that I'd thrown out the new cap she had especially bought for me, so I put the one I loved on my head and put the one I hated in the closet, behind several old sweatshirts. I went out to play wearing the first one. I played kickball with Dot Meyers next door, but she kicks cock-eyed and it was hard to see out of the cap, and when I went inside I scrounged in the closet for the second cap and it fit. That's what was so sad. It was the right size, and I put it on, and it was better. I put them both on, one after the other, because at least by size now I could tell which was which, but it was just plain true that the one I loved did not fit and kept falling off and the one they brought did fit and looked better. Dot Meyers thought I looked dumb in a bad-fitting cap, but she's dumb anyway and can't spell America right.

I saw Hannah kissing a boy I'd never seen before, outside our house, in the bushes.

That night, I put a bunch of stuff in Hannah's bedroom to freak her out, but she immediately recognized it all as mine, so it just wasn't the same.

I wore the good new cap to school.

I ate the lobster soup. I liked it. It had a neat texture. I liked it better than the usual plebeian chicken noodle my mom got. I liked the remaining wild rice one that hadn't made it into the Halloween bag; it was so hearty and different. I used the cow cup I'd salvaged from the trash, and the truth was, I liked the cow holding a balloon; it was cute. When I looked in the mirror, I sneered my upper lip and said, Benedict Arnold, Benedict Arnold, your head is on the block.

Mom came home from taking a class called Learning How to Focus Your Mind, and she seemed kind of focused, more than usual at least, and she sat with Grandma on the sofa and talked about childhood.

After a while I sat with them. There's nothing to do after homework and TV and creaming Dot Meyers.

You were a quiet child, said Grandma.

What did I like to do? asked Mom.

You liked to go with me to the store, said Grandma.

What else? asked Mom.

You liked to stir the batter, said Grandma.

What else?

I don't know, said Grandma. You liked to read.

Even as they were talking, I saw it happen on the dining room table. Saw it as they were talking, but it wasn't like an invisible hand. Just one second there was a blank table, and I blinked, and then there was a gift on the table, a red-wrapped gift with a yellow bow. It was in a box, and I went to it and sat at the table. I knew it was for me. I didn't need to tell them, plus they were talking a lot, plus Dad was at work, plus Hannah was out kissing.

It had no card, but it was really good wrapping, with those clean-cut triangular corners, and I opened it up and inside was a toy I had broken long ago. Actually, I hadn't broken it; Hannah had. It was a mouse, made of glass, and Hannah had borrowed it without asking and dropped it in the toilet by accident — so she said — and broken off the red ball nose. I had been so mad at her I hadn't spoken to her for a week and I'd made a rule that she couldn't come in my room ever again and I asked Mom for a door lock, but she didn't think I really meant it so I got one myself, at the hardware store, with a key, with money from my birthday, but I couldn't figure out how to put it on. Here was the mouse, with its nose.

What was next? Grandma?

Thanks? I said, to the air.

I took the mouse and put it on the shelf it used to be on, next to the mouse that had no nose, retrieved from the toilet. The mouse without the nose looked pathetic but a little charming, and the mouse with the nose? Well. It had never been in the toilet.

When Hannah came home, I showed her. Mom's taking a new class, I said. That's good, she said. Her face was flushed. She seemed relieved, once she paid attention, that the new mouse had arrived. Sorry about the toilet thing, she said, for the fiftieth time. It's cute, she said, patting the new one.

Let's flush it down the toilet, I said.

What?

My eyes were pleading. I could feel them, pleading.

Please, Hannah.

Hang on, she said. She went to the bathroom and splashed her face and spent a minute in there with her crushiness, and then opened up. I brought both mice in.

Both, I said, the old and the new.

Fine, she said. Whatever.

How'd you do it?

I just dropped it in, she said.

On purpose?

Yeah.

I didn't blame her. Right now, it seemed like these mice were just made for the toilet. I sat next to her on the edge of the bathtub, and dropped in the new guy. He floated around in the clean white toilet water.

Flush away, said Hannah, her eyes all shiny.

I flushed. He bobbed around and almost went down but didn't. He was slightly too big. The toilet almost overflowed. But still — the nose.

That's just what I did, she said. She was putting on lip gloss and smacking at herself in the mirror.

I picked up the wet new mouse, and broke his nose right off. It took some pressure, me holding him good in one hand and then snapping it off. You can ruin anything if you focus at it. There, I said.

I put both mice in the trash, and washed my hands. Hannah broke up with her boyfriend a few weeks later because he'd started calling her honey, and I got picked for the kickball team, and we didn't get any more gifts. Not for years.

Mom found some work downtown as a filing clerk, and Dad almost got that promotion. Hannah went to college nearby but she lived at home because of the price of rent. Grandma got older and eventually died.

When I was about to graduate high school, I did notice a packet of yellow curry in the pantry while I was rummaging around, looking for a snack. It was in a plastic yellow envelope that just said *Curry* on it in red letters. I asked my mom if she'd bought it, and she said no. Hannah? No. Dad? No. I don't like curry, I said out loud, although I'd never tried it. As an afterthought, I brought it with me to college, where I had a scholarship, so I was the first one to leave home, it turned out, and it sat in the cupboard in the dorm for four years, alongside the oregano and the salt and my roommate's birth control pills. I took it with me to my first apartment that I shared with the utilities-shirker, and my second apartment with the noxious carpet, and in my third apartment, when I was twenty-seven, living alone across the country, I opened it up one night when I was hungry and made a delicious paste with butter and milk, and then I ate it over chicken and rice and cried the whole way through it.

THE DEVOURINGS

The ogre's wife was a good woman. She was not an ogre, but she was ugly, by human standards, and she had married the ogre because he was strong and productive, and together they had made six small ogre children. The children all took after their father. She had not expected otherwise — one look at his giant teeth, height, and huge features, and she knew his genes had to be dominant.

Years earlier, she had left her own village by choice, traveling up and over the green and rising hills in search of a life for herself, and when she had met the ogre in the tavern, him stretched along the entire side wall, his voice scratched from cigar smoke, she thought she might give the alternate world a chance. Everyone in her hometown knew of the ogres, living up on Cloud Hill like that. With their magical boots, and that hen.

With also, she wondered, a range of appetites? Later that night, at his home, the ogre had been surprised at her willingness to take off her clothes, since he'd been rumored to eat people for dinner. As she unlaced her blouse, he touched fingertips to her trembling bare shoulders and explained in his low gravel that he only ate human beings he did not know. I know your name now, he murmured. I know your travels. You're safe. Her eyes were closed, and when she revealed her breasts, he sighed. They were sculpted by a different artist, he whispered to her, with a subtler tool. His desire was too much for her at first, overwhelming, but she soon grew to love him and his body, its giant harshness, its gentle gruffness with her. Next to him, she felt herself so delicate. At school, she had been the roughest-skinned, the one with the drooping features, the one no one could ever imagine that way, in a bed. She did not care about not being pretty, but she wanted to be seen as a future woman, as one who could participate, and no high-school boy could take that leap. The ogre, however, found her nothing short of revelatory, and the first time he entered her, he shouted with joy.

One evening, after many years of contented marriage, the children tucked in their bed, asleep, snoring faintly, wearing hammered gold crowns with their nightshirts because their father wanted them to feel like royal ogres in their dreams, a human girl and her siblings knocked on the door, frightened. They were lost, and the ogre was out at the tavern, and the ogre's wife opened up, and there they were — a group of six live human kids, with bright hair and red felt hats and snapping eyes, reminding her so sweetly of her long-ago nieces and nephews. The ogre's wife disliked firmly only one aspect of her husband: his interest in eating the children of humans. It could've been me! she told him once in bed while he twirled and twisted her hair over his fingers. She could not bear to turn the children out into the ogre-filled night, so she hustled them inside and in a fierce whisper told them they could hide in the same giant bed as her own children, but not to make a sound, not a peep!

When the ogre came home, late, he smelled them, of course; how could she have imagined he would not smell them? She was half-asleep, twisted in the sheets, and hoped desperately that he would just crash out on the sofa in drunkenness. What she did not know was that, earlier in the night, the smart little girl leader of the human group had swapped their six red felt hats with the six golden crowns on the heads of the deep-sleeping ogre children, and when the ogre cackled hungrily, bumbling around the house, hunting for the source of the scent, he, of poor eyesight, of booziness, of delirium, ended up eating all his own children due to the swapping of those hats.

In the early morning, the human children ran off, terrified, giggling.

We skip ahead five years, because five years were full of nothing but searing pain and tears. Five years of lying on the bed unable to move, slogging up to do the basic functioning needed to hold things together, then back to bed. Five years of scathing bitterness at ogres, and also at humans, at where she came from, and the worry that had led her to open the door; I should've let him eat them first thing! she said, weeping into the down of her pillow, though she felt sick anytime she had even gotten the hint that her husband had eaten a child. But her *own*! There were two that she mourned the most, much as she hated to admit it to herself, but she had loved Lorraine and Stillford best, the two most-complex-looking ogre faces, who had emerged post-utero like gnarled wood knots, and who had turned out to be all sweetness in nature. How they had loved their human mother. They nestled on her lap and nudged their big heads into her shoulders. They were gentle during the breastfeeding, unlike their siblings. Ogres grew teeth early, and she had to stop feeding most of them or they would've ripped off her nipple, truly. She, many times, ran to the bathroom with blood streaming from her breasts from a careless slash, a little ogre child happily lapping up the red drops on the sofa. To those she gave formula. But she was too softhearted to decide for them all; for each new child she risked her breast, and Lorraine and Stillford had been different, angled their teeth just so and suckled like little human babies, and perhaps held within their selves some of her human genes that knew not to tear at the gentleness offered. Now they were dead, digested in the system of their father, who had been so angry he split a bone out of his neck while overclenching his jaw and had to go to the hospital, where he broke four beds and injured a nurse. He was angrier than ever these days, and their marriage and its focus and tenderness had faded. His favorite had been Lutter, the super-ogre demon child, who was so kinetic she rarely saw him still, and who had scraped the walls into shreds with his nails and twice tried to swallow his mother whole. She had let him train with her husband only, and why Lutter, even in his sleep, had let himself be eaten, could only have been due to the deep dreamy trust he felt of the smell of the mouth he was entering, a mouth he knew from its firm position over his shoulder, telling him instructions on how to rip through cartilage and sinew, and an inability, due to that core of trust, to imagine his fate could end this way.

After enough time had passed, she was able to get out of bed for hours at a time. She could go to town and engage in minutes of small talk. She could sit outside on the porch and watch leaves twist on the birch trees. She could read a short article in the newsletter. On this day, a day of change, she cleaned the house, top to floor, using swaths of cloth that grew dark with dirt and dust. She swept tumbleweeds of lint out the front door, and poured scrubbing detergent into all the sinks to scour the vast yellowing basins. At the market, she bought root vegetables by the dozen and chickens and sausages. She stuffed the chickens and made a stew and fed her husband, who came

291

home ragged from his work climbing mountainsides to look for caves packed with jewels and gifts like the magical harp that that thief Jack had stolen from his brother years ago.

We are pillaged, constantly, said the ogre, laying his loot in a sparkling heap by the door. And they fear us?

He kissed her on the ear, and sat down to roll a cigar out of crisp brown paper and a fist-sized wad of tobacco.

Good stew, human, he said, after dinner.

Please don't call me that, she said, for the hundredth time.

That's right, he said, patting his belly. I'm sorry. Love that sausage, delicious. He lit the cigar and inhaled deeply.

She wiped the globs of leftover chicken off the dining room table with a sponge.

While he mumbled to himself, digesting, sleepy, she filled the pots with soap and water to soak, and ate a little bowl of the chicken stew behind the counter. She rarely ate at the same table as her husband anymore, as she now feared him during mealtimes, couldn't stand to watch him slurp up animals with that vigor and those grinding, pointed teeth.

Husband, she said, putting her bowl aside. She walked out from behind the counter. I have decided I need to go on a trip, she said.

The ogre was finishing his fourth mug of wine. He liked the darkest wine, the red almost black.

Go where? he said, wiping his mouth. To see your family?

She shook her head. Her family lived below, in the people village, and last time she'd been home, before the devourings, everyone had lectured her on ogres and complicity and betrayal. She'd waved them off. He's a good one, she had said. She had not dared show pictures of her children.

I'd like to see something pretty, she said. Maybe a lake?

There's a river that's supposed to be nice a few valleys over, he said, exhaling bracelets of smoke to the rafters.

Okay, she said. A river.

I could go with you, he said, turning a giant brown eye to hers. His eye like a pool hers could swim inside.

A mucky pool.

No, she told him. I need to do this alone.

He nodded. He understood. They both coped in their own ways. He had women on the side, ogre women, everyone knew. Maybe she didn't know, but probably. After all, although being with a human was the ultimate in showing off both self-control and status, sometimes a man just wanted a woman like himself. There were no prostitutes in the ogre village, as it was a barter economy and females chose males with equal discernment, but there were a couple who liked this particular ogre, and every few months he'd make a little sojourn as a way to honor where he came from. It's for my mother, he told his ogre-woman once, and she'd laughed and laughed, nude and mottled and calm, sprawled over a mattress, one arm crossing loosely over her forehead.

The ogre helped his wife pack up. He buttoned up her bag and told her he would miss her, which was true. From his plunder, he gave her a magic cloak that would turn her into the color of the dappled light that shot through foliage, and also a cake that would become more cake once she'd eaten half. He kissed her forehead, roughly, and she melted a little under his arms.

Do you know how long you'll be? he asked.

I don't know, she said.

Okay, he said. I'll be here.

They spent the night almost close, her forehead pressed against the wall of his triceps. Come morning, she walked through the door and into fields of glistening green.

■ ■ ■ ■

What marriage could recover? She did not plan on ever returning. The ogre wasn't sure, but he thought it was unlikely. He was not insensitive, despite all suspicions. The day she left, he skipped work and went to the tavern for lunch and drank ninety-five beers. You're a machine! the other ogres said, admiringly, as he slammed down another stein. Foam made an old man's beard around his mouth, and he burped in an echo that trembled the hillsides.

She felt it, his wife, now miles away, following a winding path up and over lightly rolling hills covered in sage, and dandelion fields, and one meadow of sunflowers shuddering in the daylight. She walked and walked until dusk, trying to collect distance under her feet, and then she camped out under a shady elm with her checkered cloth. She unpacked some almonds and dried cherries and she also ate the cake, which would let itself diminish to half and then, under her bare eyes, build itself back up out of nothing, out of air, until it was a full cake again. She was grateful for it, but somehow it also bothered her. Finish, cake, she said, tearing off half, watching it rebuild. Finish!

She tore off more than half, the whole, but the cake was unstoppable. Plus, she needed it. What, she was going to trap birds and roast them over a fire? She was a woman who shopped at a market with a wheeled cart and used honey-lavender soap. She drank from her water mug and refilled it at a spring at the edge of the meadow, and before she fell asleep, she sprinkled the remaining cake crumbs around her cloth.

In the morning, she awoke surrounded by expectant-looking crows. Enough! she said, shaking the cloth as they tottered away.

Really, she could've spent the rest of her life there, just sitting and feeding those crows and herself with the cake, but she wanted to reach the river.

When she heard a clip-clopping sound, she put on the cloak so that she looked like the dappled sunlight beneath the elm, a particularly glorious sunlit area that did not correspond to the rules of sun location in the sky, but who would notice that except a particularly astute observer of shadows? This was just a human horseman riding along in ogre country, looking to find some treasure, like his comrades who had come up here and survived. She watched him, his handsomeness, his vanity and sureness, his sculpted hair and cheeks, his strong hands, his proud red jacket, and she was reminded again why the ogres had attracted her, and why she had loved young Stillford so, his wet brown eyes searching out hers, those sharp, smiling, crooked teeth. The ogres knew they were ugly and in that they were decent. They did not ever think they could be like this man, she thought as he galloped off, tossing his head with pleasure. He ducked and rose over hills, and she saw it coming before he did, saw the ogre who ran the corner store just out on a pleasant walk in his seven-league boots, rounding the corner and — surprise! what a gift! — the man too late raising his gun and landing a shot on the ogre's shoulder, which was nothing to an ogre, nothing a little mending at night wouldn't fix, a little digging with a fork into flesh to expunge a bullet, and she watched in her cloak as the man was plucked from his horse and eaten whole. It was a horrible sight, one she had tried not to see for most of her wedded life, but on that day she found it almost comforting. Just to see it. Not comforting to see pain and death but just to see what she could not let herself imagine and therefore ruled her. She wept quietly under the tree as the ogre chewed. Then he walked off, rubbing his belly, wearing those boots, a little scrap of red cloth sticking out of his mouth until he reached out a tongue and licked it in, just like a human might do with a bit of jam.

The horse had run off, but it circled back after the ogre left, pacing in the field, then settling down, and after her shaking subsided, she walked over to where it was grazing. A couple of hours had passed, and the horse seemed focused on the grass, and calm. After all, the eating had been brief, and the man had barely had time to scream, and ogres were just about food, not about power play or torture. They were just endlessly large and hungry beings. She mounted the horse and rode lazily along, digging around in the thick leather packs on the side where she found some snacks — turkey jerky that she used to love, made in the village, and some peaches, a rare delicacy for her, as ogres couldn't care less about peaches, and the fragrance consumed her mouth, like eating perfume, like kisses of nectar. She found a letter from a wife in royal-blue ink from a quill pen, wishing the man well. It was all awful, she thought, tossing the peach stone onto the green hillside, where it wedged against a rock, near some bees. Happy bees. She patted the horse's neck. Now she and the widow had something in common. Though loss did not pass from one person to another like a baton; it just formed a bigger and bigger pool of carriers. And, she thought, scratching the coarseness of the horse's mane, it did not leave once lodged, did it, simply changed form and asked repeatedly for attention and care, as each year revealed a new knot to cry out and consider — smaller, sure, but never gone. Stillford, she thought to herself, as the sun grew high in the sky. My sweet Stillford, with his dirt art. My funny Lorraine, who danced to the lute so earnestly. Out of my body, these beautiful monsters.

It was ridiculous, at times, how many tears one body could produce.

A few hours into the afternoon, during a nap on the horse, who was eating clover in the inverted bell of a valley, the ring of trumpets awoke the woman. She jerked awake, recalling the sound from her childhood, when trumpets were the way news was delivered, and sure enough, across the field emerged a troop of human men and women on horseback, some walking, two trumpeting, one waving a bright-red flag. From what she could recall, a bright-red flag meant war.

Ho, woman! called the strapping man at

the lead, and she did not have time to put on her cloak; even if she had, they'd take her horse, and she liked having the horse.

They trotted over, a whole mess of people, and she hadn't looked at so many human faces together in years. How refined they were! How tiny and delicate! Those dot nostrils! Their hairless hands!

Are you lost? the head man asked, not unkindly. He wore a helmet wrought with silver swirled markings on the sides that seemed to speak of royalty.

No, she said, thank you. I'm on my way to the river.

This is ogre territory! said the man, sitting straighter. You're not safe!

He turned to the others, beckoning them closer.

No, no, she said, waving him off. It's fine. I'm skilled at hiding. I've been living in this territory for years.

Ho! he said, digging his hands into his horse's mane. Years? And survived? You must help us, then! We sent out a scout earlier to look for mines, and we have not heard back. Did you see anyone?

Of course, one careful look at the horse and all would be revealed, but the man was very focused on her face, as if he had been trained in it.

No, she said.

You saw no danger? said the man.

Nothing but crows, she said.

Ogres *eat* people, said the man, leaning in.

To her annoyance, her eyes thickened with tears.

Ah! You've seen something?

She shook her head, tucking her hands under the saddle and feeling the horse's warm coat beneath her, the large and living backside. No. I just heard a story once, of someone getting eaten, and I found it sad, she said. The tears tracked her cheeks.

He nodded. They all had their own stories.

Our sentry is a good man, the man said, and he said he'd contact us immediately via light signaling with use of the sun and his mirror and we have not seen a thing. Ah! Is that his horse?

He glanced down, and saw the packs. She had in her lap some turkey jerky that she'd been eating earlier.

Oh, I don't know! she said. She widened her eyes. Is it? I was just walking and came upon this horse and needed a rest. Hours ago. It did not have an owner.

The man's brow furrowed. The horse, alone? Hours ago?

Alone, she said.

He consulted with a short man next to him on a taller horse, making them even.

You'll have to come with us, the main man said.

Oh no, she said, slipping the turkey jerky into a pocket. I'll walk. I'll give you his horse. I didn't realize it belonged to anyone recently. I thought it had been wild for a while.

No, said the man, firmly. We need you to come with us.

He gave a nod to his short man, who began to dismount.

The woman leapt off her horse, and backed into the meadow. The afternoon sun filtered through pine needles on high fir trees to the side, and with a quick move she had the cloak out of her bag and on and had turned into light and shadow.

Where'd she go? said the short man.

Witch! said the first.

The trumpets raised and blared.

The woman crept quietly to a corner of the meadow. Had any one of them been attuned to light, they would've seen one patch of splattered sun shapes moving along in a way that did not correspond to the breeze.

But they were not. They were preoccupied with what had happened. They had liked their handsome, courageous scout. They

302

quickly assimilated the man's packs and letters into their crew, and put a child who had been previously riding with his mother onto the horse, and the two lead men swore, and the woman watched silently from her spot in the meadow as they moved in a clump over the hills.

She stayed in the meadow in the cloak for hours, and the sun went down and lit the grasses with orange light, and she wondered about her husband, who was likely going to see one of his women on the side. Although it made her cringe inside, a fist in her stomach, there was also a distant relief in it, in people just doing what they needed to do. She found comfort in the way the grasses swayed, and murmured, and at dinner-time, in a little whisper, she asked the cake to change flavor, and, magic cake that it was, it shifted from vanilla pound to a chocolate Bundt, and she ate it with pleasure, plus some more almonds she had in her pocket and the remaining turkey jerky. Water from the spring. The moon rose in a crescent and crickets rubbed their wings together and in the far distance, now and again, she could hear the shining bleats of the bugles and trumpets.

■ ■ ■ ■

In the morning, she walked on. She could smell the river now, the heavy moisture, the damper grasses under her feet. The trumpets had grown fainter, and she imagined they were returning home to arm up and come back to try to defeat the ogres with guns and bayonets. Maybe they will, she thought, vaguely, though the ogres had magic and bigness on their side, and the humans had a hubris ogres did not. Ogres bumbled, and erred, but their weaknesses were not hidden, and this helped them, in the long run.

She ate her lunch (more dried cherries) and then took the cake out of her bag. Something about it still bothered her. I need to fight for my life a little harder than this, she told it. It was now a chocolate chip cake, and she felt bad for it, this cake so willing to change and please her, with no other beings around who could speak to it, and enjoy it, but she ate a small portion and then wrapped it in a checkered napkin and tucked it in the branched fork of a sturdy oak.

Here, cake, she told it, patting the napkin. You are to have your own adventure now.

No matter what happens, you can grow again.

As she said it, as she stooped to shoulder her bag, she understood why she could not tolerate being around a cake that survived so repeatedly, and she stood, bowed at the branch, and walked away.

Finding food became much harder then. She rooted for berries, having learned years ago from her husband what was edible, but more times than not, the berries were bad. She ate a handful of sour ones in the afternoon, and dug up some old peanuts and a beet. Dirt filled the cracks in her hands. She found a strong stick and rubbed the end to a point with the paring knife she'd brought in her sack, and when she finally reached the river — dark blue, racing, stone-dribbled — after refilling her water (ogre-country water was always drinkable — something to do with the deep reserves replenished by the clouds), she saw a quick orange fish in the current and crouched down and, after dozens of tries, speared it. The fish flapped on her stick, and she knelt and prayed a thank you. She had only seen a fire built in front of her a few times, but she was able to wrangle together some sticks and fir needles and

305

with the matches she had in her pack managed to get enough going to scorch the cleaned fish, though she missed many of the bones and picked them from her teeth in thin pullings. She let the fish guts molder in the grasses for another animal. Everything would get eaten in some way or another.

She slept that night wearing the cloak, a bright spot of dapple in the darkness. Soon into her sleep, she woke at the sound of rustling, and caught a bear cub next to her licking up the fish guts and eyeing her sunspot curiously. She removed the cloak and it scampered away. The next morning, she wrapped up the cloak and left it in another tree's branches. She did not want help from magic. She did not want any more handouts.

She grew rugged and wiry in the fields, spearing fish, using up the last of her matches but not until she was sure she had figured out how to make a fire on her own, which sometimes took over an hour. Her legs turned leaner and tanner, and she squatted and watched the clouds and the river and felt her sense of internal time shifting. We adapt, she told herself repeatedly. This is what they mean by adaptable. The men rose up from the village with their spears and guns, and when she saw the glints of red and the banners of war she climbed a high tree and watched from a distance as the human forces with shining weaponry and brass charged into ogre territory. Into the thatched huts and the rickety tavern and the ogre game-field full of nets and balls woven from goat hide. She watched, again, as the ogres ate the men whole. They could eat and eat. She watched the ogres fall from the expert weaponry, and the sight of a fallen ogre enraged the other ogres and invigorated the remaining men, so the last phase was particularly bloody. Casualties were tossed off an embankment on Cloud Hill, and far below, people cried out and ran from the falling bodies.

On one of the days, she spotted her husband from the height of her best scouting tree, near the widest part of the river, where she'd set up a little daily life for herself that included hours of watching insects move grasses around or feeling the wind shift over her skin. Her husband, who had aged. She could see it in his limp. She missed him. She felt from his limp that he missed her. She had taken good care of him. He had been her one and only love. She watched as he swiped at the humans with swinging arms and ate two and then stumbled off and could not continue. The humans shot guns in his direction but he just swatted bullets like sport and the humans were radically outnumbered by that point and her ogre was one of the biggest. He limped farther away, and then twisted and turned, and his body moved in a way she'd never seen before, an uncomfortable jerking, an insistent movement from feet up to mouth, and he vomited up human — legs and arms and a head tumbled straight out of him. It was unchewed, the body — it was just parts and parcels of humanness — and the pieces lay there in the grass, glazed in a layer of spit and acid. Everyone stopped, for a second, seeing that: the man who had not been chewed, but had been split into parts, and was of course dead. The ogres held still, sweating, staring. The ogres had never seen an ogre throw anything up in their lives; they were nothing if not able digesters, and they shuddered at the sight of it.

On light feet, the woman crept closer. She ran through the grasses and leapt into another tree. The humans were muttering amongst themselves because although they had seen bodies eaten it was something else to see a body reemerge. The man's parts were now moldering in the grass, perhaps for the same bear cub. When she was close

308

enough, at a high perch, she found she could recognize the man. An uncle of hers, a distant uncle, her mother's eldest brother. His twisted hand, his nose, that tweaked shoulder and distinctive jaw. She clung to the branch and thought perhaps her husband had thrown up the man because the taste had reminded him of his own children. Perhaps he had banged up against memory through an inexplicable familiarity. He had never told her he was sad. He had never expressed true regret. They had, in fact, never really talked about it. How to talk about it? How could she blame him, or could he blame her? Weren't they both to blame for it, and also blameless? Who were the little human children who'd escaped, and where were they now?

The remaining ogres staggered off, and the remaining humans went to surround her dead uncle's parts. It was a truce moment. There had been enough death, and the ogres were not going to be vanquished, and the remaining humans did not want to be eaten, so they put the uncle's body into burlap bags and began the slow march home. Her ogre sank to the grasses on his knees and hung his head. He stayed there for hours, wilted, hunched, and from her perch in the tree, she sent him love. She made her love into a piece of the wind, formed from the air in her and placed on the air outside her, and sent it to him, even though it would be too diffuse by the time it got there. Still, even the bear cub felt it, trotting over to whatever remaining organ bits he could find, lifting up his nose to smell the new hint of freshness in the evening air.

The cake, at first, had remained in the tree. Lodged in the branch nook of the old oak where she'd left it. But various birds found it in a few short days — they could smell its bready sweetness from yards away — and they pecked so hard at the napkin that the cake fell from the nook and rolled out of the linen. On the ground, the birds pecked it into nothing. It replenished. They pecked. It replenished. The cake wanted to satisfy the birds, so it made itself into a seeded type, and the birds went at it with new vigor. The cake replenished. The birds were so full they hopped off, wobbling, but they returned with eagerness in the morning, and the next morning, and the birds that lived near the oak tree became fat and listless. They could hardly fly. All they did all day long was peck at the cake.

The cake had grown old. It had been

made so many years ago, and it had been so many cakes in its time.

I will never die, thought the cake to itself, in even simpler terms, as cakes did not have sophisticated use of language.

On her walk back, the woman saw it on the ground. She recognized her napkin, checked blue against the dirt. She was heading home. She was not sure if she could really return, or how to do it, but she wanted to try. She missed her husband, and the sight of him throwing up her uncle had filled her with a sore and tender love. There was the cake, in seeded form now, and she felt sorry for it.

With her pointed stick, she dug a hole in the ground. Now, dear cake, she said, gently burying it, patting the dirt. At least you can rest. At least you will not be endlessly pecked and diminished.

The birds found it in a day. A cake like that? Let that kind of thing go? They thought not. They scrabbled in the dirt and dragged it out with their beaks. They had missed it, for that missing day. They pecked with unusual ardor. A few worms had already attached to its bottom side and were eating it too, and the cake had formed its back side into a kind of dirt cake and its front into seed, and it would replenish itself according to the ratio of its eaters.

It went on like this for a while, and a few of the birds died early, from overeating and lack of flight. New birds came and went. Same with the worms.

The woman returned to her house, and her husband opened the door, widening it when he saw it was her, and they sat at the kitchen table. It did not feel wrong. She got up and took her items out of her dirty bag and piled them into the sink for laundry. That moment a few days later when their arms touched over by the guest room? They ate their stew bowls together. They walked formally into the living room, sat on a sofa, and stumbled through a conversation. At night, she climbed onto his chest to sleep and he held her in place like a belt. Later, they took a few trips to a waterfall, and a glacier, and befriended an ogre who ran a school. After many years, the woman died of natural causes, and a few years after that, the ogre died. Eventually, his mistresses died. Down on the ground, in the people village, over decades, the war men and women died. The human girl who had escaped her early death died, across the land, over by the ocean, in her shack of blue bowls and rocking chairs. The witch who had originally made the cake and made up the spell and given it as a gift to her beloved ogre-friend died.

The cake went on and on.

Time passed, and the climate shifted. The trees and grasses faded, and the land grew dry. Birds stopped flying overhead. Reptiles ate the cake but eventually died out. The worms dried into dust. A quarter mile away, the magic cloak had stayed stuffed in its tree, hidden from view over many, many years. Some wind had nudged it into open air, and now, half-tucked in the broken branches of a dead tree trunk, was a shining bright coat-shaped area of dappled light through foliage. It showed dapple long after the sun had stopped shining through any leaves, because there were no more leaves.

Neither could move, but the cake felt a sense of the presence of the cloak, and thought it might be a new eater coming to find the cake, and the cake, always wanting to please — the cake who had found a way to survive its endlessness by recreating its role over and over again — tried to figure out in its cake way what this light-dappled object might want to eat. So it became darkness. A cake of darkness. It did not have to be human food. It did not have to be digestible through a familiar tract. It lay there on the dirt, waiting, a shimmering cake of darkness. Through time, and wind, and earthquakes, and chance, at last the cloak fell out of the tree and blew across the land and happened upon the cake, where it ate its darkness and extinguished its own dappled light. The cloak disappeared into night and was not seen again, as it was only a piece of coat-shaped darkness now and could no longer be spotted so easily, had there been any eyes left to see it. It floated and joined with nowhere. Darkness was overtaking everything anyway. Pouring over the land and sky. The cake itself, still in the shape of darkness, sat on the hillside.

What's left? said the cake. It thought in blocks of feeling. It felt the thick darkness all around it. What is left to eat me? To take me in?

Darkness did not want to eat more darkness, not especially. Darkness did not care for carrot cake, or apple pie. Darkness did not seem interested in a water cake, or a cake of money. Only when the cake filled with light did it come over. The darkness, circling around the light, devouring the light. But the cake kept refilling, as we know. This is the spell of the cake. And the darkness, eating light, and again light, and again light, lifted.

ACKNOWLEDGMENTS

Big thanks to the core of usual suspects, including Bill Thomas and Henry Dunow, Coralie Hunter and Yishai Seidman and Mark Miller, plus additional indebtedness for new help and advisement from Sarah Bynum, Mark Danielewski, Susan Laemmle, and Amy Cutler for her wonderfully evocative painting *Tiger Mending.*

I'd also like to express my deep appreciation to the various editors at magazines and literary journals and anthologies and radio shows who are true champions of the short story. Including, but of course not just: Kate Bernheimer, John Siciliano, Andy Hunter, Halimah Marcus, Steve Erickson, Rob Spillman, Win McCormack, Will Allison, Hannah Tinti, Matthew Fishbane, Dave Eggers, Jordan Bass, Brock Clarke, Nicola Mason, Katherine Minton, the late Isaiah Sheffer, Lydia Ship, Chloe Plaunt, Jim Shepard, Steven Lee Beeber, Adrian Todd Zuniga,

Jeff VanderMeer, Sumanth Prabhaker, Nathaniel Rich, Aaron Hicklin, David Milofsky, Bob Fogarty, Wendy Lesser, and Lee Montgomery.

The stories in this collection were previously published, sometimes in slightly different form, in the following publications: "Appleless" in *The Fairy Tale Review;* "The Red Ribbon" in *Electric Literature;* "Tiger Mending" — based on an Amy Cutler painting — first in *Black Book* and then in *Best American Non-Required Reading;* "Faces" in *The Paris Review;* "On a Saturday Afternoon" in *nerve.com* and *Black Clock;* "The Fake Nazi" in *Ploughshares;* "Lemonade" and "Americca" in *Tin House;* "Bad Return" in *One Story;* "Origin Lessons" on *Studio 360* and in *The Chattahoochee Review;* "The Doctor and the Rabbi" in *Tablet;* "Wordkeepers" in *McSweeney's;* "The Color Master" in *The Cincinnati Review* and *My Mother She Killed Me, My Father He Ate Me* (New York: Penguin Books, 2010); "A State of Variance" in

Awake! A Reader for the Sleepless and *Opium;* and "The Devourings" forthcoming in an anthology of new myths from Penguin.

ABOUT THE AUTHOR

Aimee Bender is the author of the novels *The Particular Sadness of Lemon Cake,* a national bestseller, and *An Invisible Sign of My Own* and of the collections *The Girl in the Flammable Skirt* and *Willful Creatures.* Her work has been widely anthologized and has been translated into sixteen languages. She lives in Los Angeles.